MUSEUM OF MYSTERIES

QUARTZING TROUBLE

Margaret Welch

Annie's
AnniesFiction.com

Books in the Museum of Mysteries series

Mummy's the Word
Buried Secrets
Doubloon Jeopardy
Naughty or Knife
Final Resting Vase
Out of the Picture
Caught Redheaded
Do or Diamond
Rotten to the Encore
Artifact or Fiction
Quartzing Trouble

... and more to come!

Quartzing Trouble
Copyright © 2022 Annie's.

All rights reserved. No part of this publication may be reproduced, stored in a retrieval system, or transmitted in any form or by any means—electronic, mechanical, photocopying, recording or otherwise—without the prior written permission of the publisher. The only exception is brief quotations in printed reviews. For information address Annie's, 306 East Parr Road, Berne, Indiana 46711-1138.

The characters and events in this book are fictional, and any resemblance to actual persons or events is coincidental.

Library of Congress Cataloging-in-Publication Data
Quartzing Trouble / by Margaret Welch
p. cm.
I. Title
2022941572

AnniesFiction.com
(800) 282-6643
Museum of Mysteries™
Series Creators: Shari Lohner and Lorie Jones
Series Editor: Marci Clark

10 11 12 13 14 | Printed in China | 9 8 7 6 5 4 3 2 1

1

"Wait. Did you hear that?" Scarlett McCormick put her hand on Winnie Varma's arm. They stopped walking toward the special exhibits gallery and listened. From other parts of the Reed Museum of Art and Archaeology, visitors' voices filtered to them. Footsteps echoed on the marble floors. But there was something else. "There it is again," Scarlett said. "There's a bird making noises in the gallery."

"*Something's* in the gallery," Winnie said, "but it doesn't sound like any bird I've ever heard."

"Not a little songbird, anyway," Scarlett said.

Cautiously, the two women continued toward the closed gallery. As the museum's head curator and head of security, they'd planned to do a final walk-through of the new *Art from the Golden Age of Illustration* exhibit Scarlett had mounted in the gallery. The exhibit featured original works by Florence Harrison, Jessie Willcox Smith, Maxfield Parrish, Norman Rockwell, and N. C. Wyeth, among others. With the exhibit's opening night party slated for that evening, Scarlett and Winnie were eager to find and eliminate any last-minute problems.

And even a small bird in a museum filled with priceless art and artifacts is a big *problem,* Scarlett thought.

Folding screens on wheels, each with a poster advertising the new exhibit, created a barrier across the gallery's broad opening. A row of crowd-control stanchions with ropes were positioned in front of the folding screens, emphasizing that the exhibit wasn't yet open to the public. As Scarlett and Winnie approached the stanchions and screens, the whistling started again.

"It can't be a bird," Winnie said. "The loading dock is the only way one could possibly get in. If a bird *did* come in that way, there's no way it could get past all the closed doors from the dock on the lower level to here on the first floor."

"I like your confidence," Scarlett said. "But if it's not a bird, then that means someone's here who shouldn't be. Let's find out who." Scarlett adjusted the sleeves of her blazer and tucked her waves of red hair behind her ears. She and Winnie skirted the barriers so they could see into the gallery.

A young woman wearing a pink knitted beanie sat cross-legged on a bench in front of the Wyeth paintings. She worked with a pencil on a large sketchpad, darting glances at a painting from *Treasure Island* on the wall in front of her.

"Did you give her permission to be here?" Winnie whispered.

The young woman suddenly whistled a shrill birdcall.

"That whistle was actually painful," Scarlett said. "No, I didn't give her permission. I recognize her, though. She came in Monday and asked if she could get into the exhibit early."

"Well, let's go tell her she's still too early."

They walked into the room. The young woman was either so engrossed in her work that she didn't hear their footsteps, or she chose to ignore them.

"Earbuds," Winnie said.

Scarlett and Winnie walked around in front of the young woman so that they stood between her and the painting.

"Rylla, isn't it?" Scarlett said. "Rylla Summers?"

The young woman raised her head, pinning Scarlett with her striking blue eyes. "Summerville, actually. Rylla Villa would be cool, though, wouldn't it?" She squinted at her work, then rubbed out a line and redrew it.

Winnie leaned forward. "We're sorry to interrupt you, Ms. Summerville—"

"Then don't."

"I beg your pardon?" Winnie asked, clearly taken aback.

"Have you ever been an art student? Do you know how many pieces they expect us to produce? It's endless. The instructor goes on and on about the importance of copying the masters."

Scarlett frowned. "I told you Monday that the exhibit isn't open to the public."

"I know, and I'm sorry, but I needed to work alone." Rylla didn't seem especially repentant.

"The exhibit opens Saturday," Winnie said. "Tomorrow."

Rylla sighed heavily. She flipped her sketchpad closed and put her pencils and eraser in a case that she slipped into her backpack. "Some of the other illustrators in here—Jessie Willcox Smith, for instance—are like spun sugar. But Wyeth's stuff is so cool, and I just wanted time alone with it."

"Come back tomorrow," Scarlett said.

"And Sunday?"

"We aren't open Sundays, but we'll be happy to see you all next week."

"It'll be crowded tomorrow and next week. What about tonight? For your party?"

"We're expecting a crowd tonight too," Winnie said. "And it's exclusively for donors and members."

"Riffraff refused?"

"I didn't mean it that way," Winnie said.

"No worries. It wouldn't bother me even if you did."

"There's plenty more art on this floor and upstairs," Scarlett said. "You're welcome to work anywhere else but here for today."

"Okay, maybe." Rylla hiked her backpack onto one shoulder and tucked her drawing pad under her arm.

Scarlett and Winnie followed her toward the opening in the barrier. As she reached the exit, Rylla faced them and pulled off her beanie, revealing her hair buzz-cut into a pattern of feathers. The feathers were dyed iridescent green with hints of blue at her crown shading into bright violet around her ears and nape.

Rylla gave them a shallow curtsey. "May the rest of your afternoon be agreeable, and may you have no more unpleasant surprises before your fancy party this evening."

When Rylla had disappeared around the corner, Winnie asked, "Should I follow her to make sure she leaves?"

"No. As long as she stays out of here, she's fine. Let's do a walk-through of the space again after we close this afternoon."

"I'll add it to my list. Question, though," Winnie said. "What did she mean by that? What she said about wishing us no more unpleasant surprises before the party tonight. How did that strike you?"

"Kind of odd, but consider the source," Scarlett said. "She'd already been told the exhibit is off-limits, but she went in anyway."

"Good point. But I'm also considering my training as a security officer."

"She sneaked in, then sat there practicing birdcalls, which wasn't sneaky at all. It's like she *wanted* us to find her. Unless whistling birdcalls is a habit, and she didn't realize she was doing it."

"No, between the birdcalls and the feathered head, I think she likes calling attention to herself," Winnie said.

"Her hair was kind of cool."

"It was."

Scarlett eyed her. "You don't sound convinced."

"Of her hair?" Winnie asked. "Oh, sure. It's very cool. My parents would be appalled if *I* ever did that, but that's not what I meant."

"You're fishing for something. You noticed something odd and you want to know if I noticed as well."

"We're so often on the same wavelength." Winnie made a show of studying Scarlett's forehead. "Yeah, I see another thought in there."

Scarlett grimaced. "I feel ridiculous saying it, but okay. Her wish that we have no more unpleasant surprises sounded like a wish from a bad fairy in a Grimm brothers' tale."

"Excellent. We are on the same wavelength. That makes me feel better, because I thought I might be overreacting. We still might be, but what she said, and the way she said it, sounded an awful lot like a threat."

Scarlett took her lunch outside to enjoy it in the museum's gardens. Devon Reed, the late founder of the Reed Museum of Art and Archaeology, had had an eye for more than antiquities and beautiful artwork. He'd chosen the grand Spanish revival building in charming Crescent Harbor, California, to house his collections. Then he'd surrounded the building with gardens perfect for strolling, meditating, and enjoying late lunches.

After finishing her sandwich, Scarlett closed her eyes and tilted her face toward the sun. Then she heard two familiar voices.

"Why, Hal," Greta Baron said. "It's a sunflower."

"You're right," Hal answered. "The rare and remarkable redheaded sunflower, harbinger of Crescent Harbor's golden time of year."

Scarlett laughed and opened her eyes to see Greta and Hal Baron walking toward her, arm in arm. The Barons, both retired professors from nearby Santa Catalina College, were the Reed's main docents. Greta had taught history. Hal had taught theater.

As they approached, Scarlett asked, "Why is September Crescent Harbor's 'golden time of year'?"

"It's when the autumn wildflowers lend their golden glow," Hal said. "Behold the lizard tail yarrow and seaside painted cup." He pointed out two beds of yellow and orange blooms. "So clever of you to arrange the *Art from the Golden Age of Illustration* exhibit to coincide with all this glory."

"It's a nice way to mark the upcoming end of my first year at the Reed too," Scarlett said.

"A year?"

"Next month," Scarlett clarified.

"That's amazing," Greta said.

"Assessment time, then," Hal said. "Are you glad you took the job?"

Scarlett had fallen in love with Crescent Harbor at first sight. She and Cleo, her cat, felt completely at home in their Mission Revival-style house. She no longer questioned whether she was up for the job as head curator, and was confident she'd made the right decision leaving New York behind. "Best decision in the world. Cleo thinks so too."

A bird sang, as if agreeing with Scarlett. Or was it Rylla? No, it was definitely a bird. It actually knew how to sing.

"Do you know what kind of bird that is?" Scarlett asked.

"A golden-crowned sparrow," Greta said.

"Thanks." Scarlett stood and stretched. "I better get back to it." She waved to the docents, then went back inside and stopped at Burial Grounds in the lobby.

"You seem serene." Allie Preston, who ran the coffee shop, handed a cup to Scarlett. "That's a fine accomplishment mere hours before an opening event."

"I love this exhibit, and the opening will be fun. And for once, I'm actually confident that everything is in order."

"I'm sorry I'll miss it, but the waves are irresistible today." Allie kissed her fingertips like a professional chef. She lived to surf, and according to her, September brought perfect ocean swells. Allie's smile always reminded Scarlett of California sunshine, but then her face clouded over. "I don't usually think of unusual as a problem, but there was a woman here today who was a bit . . ." Her face went from cloudy to uncomfortable.

"Unusual?" Scarlett asked.

Allie's discomfort disappeared with another smile, though by Allie-standards the smile was subdued. "I'm not entirely sure why I think she might be a problem, but I got the feeling she *wanted* to be a problem."

"You're speaking in riddles."

"You like mysteries."

"I do, but that whole serenity thing you noticed is riding on there being no mysteries and no problems tonight."

"Gotcha," Allie said. "It was her laugh that caught my attention. She laughed as she came from the Ancient American gallery, and she laughed all the way through the lobby to the door. I like a good laugh, but this laugh seemed like a private joke and a dare at the same time. Like if anyone had thought her laugh was contagious and joined in, then she would've stopped and given them the stink eye. But I also got the feeling she *wanted* someone to laugh with her, or to shush her, so she *could* give them the stink eye."

"That's a lot to get from someone laughing on their way out the door."

"I'm good at the nuances of laughter."

"I believe it. Can you describe the person laughing as well as you did the laugh?" Scarlett asked.

"Twenty-ish," Allie said. "A few inches taller than I am. A few shorter than you. She had a backpack and a large drawing pad." She mimed the pad's dimensions with her hands.

Scarlett tried not to groan. "What about her hair?"

"Tucked up under a pink beanie."

"Not tucked," Scarlett said. "You'd love it. She has a buzz cut done in a pattern of feathers and dyed in shades of green with some blue and purple."

Allie put a hand to her own head as if picturing the look. "Wow. So you know who I'm talking about?"

"Let's say I'm aware of her," Scarlett said. "So is Winnie. Her name is Rylla Summerville. When you saw her, was she just laughing, or did she make birdcalls?"

"Birdcalls? Okay, I'm changing my description of this woman from 'unusual' to 'interesting, tending toward eccentric.' Maybe she wasn't laughing. She might've been imitating Woody Woodpecker."

"You're a nut," Scarlett said. "And let's hope Rylla isn't."

"Good plan. Sorry about the bobble in your serenity, but I'll leave Rylla's eccentric ways for you to fathom, and I'll go paddle out a hundred fathoms or so to catch my perfect wave."

"Fathoms are depth, though," Scarlett said. "Please go for distance instead. I don't want to think about you disappearing into the depths."

The museum closed at two on Fridays. At three, Scarlett stood in the lobby going over her pre-event checklist one more time.

Second walk-through of the exhibit space—done.

Remove barriers from gallery entrance—done.

Caterers—due to arrive at four, two hours before the event.

Jazz trio—also due to arrive at four.
Run home, change clothes, and placate Cleo.

"Are we on schedule?" Greta asked. She and Hal had volunteered to help that afternoon before running home to change.

"Believe it or not, I think we're in great shape," Scarlett replied.

Winnie came toward them with a book-size package. Scarlett's breath caught at the worry etched between Winnie's eyebrows.

"I'm glad I caught all three of you," Winnie said. "The mail carrier dropped this off at the loading dock. Does the name Quartz Sutton ring any bells?"

"None at all," Scarlett said.

"Not for me either." Greta looked at Hal who shook his head.

"This is addressed to Quartz Sutton, in care of Greta and Hal Barron—misspelled with two Rs instead of one—in care of the museum," Winnie said. "It's marked 'private.'"

"Beside the fact that we aren't likely to forget a name like Quartz," Hal said, "we would never take advantage of the museum by suggesting a mailing arrangement like that."

"Is this an 'unpleasant surprise'?" Scarlett asked.

"That's what I'm wondering," Winnie said. "It has a return address of Larkfield, California. Do you know anyone there?"

"Not that I'm aware of," Greta said.

"I've never even heard of Larkfield," Hal said.

"*Lark*field. Is that suspicious, or do I simply have birds on the brain?" Scarlett asked.

"We can end the suspense easily enough." Hal reached for the package.

"No." Winnie took a step back. "First, it isn't addressed to any of us. Second, misspelled names and restrictive markings are some of the indicators for identifying suspicious packages. And earlier today, we had an odd warning about unpleasant surprises."

"From someone whistling birdcalls, with her hair cut and dyed to resemble feathers," Scarlett added.

Winnie set the package carefully on the floor. "So, out of an abundance of caution, let's all step away from it, because there's a chance that it contains something unpleasant or even dangerous, like a toxin or an explosive."

2

"Poison? Explosives?" Greta stared at the package sitting on the lobby floor. "Aren't those possibilities an extreme leap to make from 'unpleasant surprises'? Is there any reason to believe the package contains something dangerous? Why would the museum be a target? Why would Hal and I be targets?"

"Greta," Hal said gently but firmly. "These things happen. Now's not the time to debate the logic behind a possible catastrophe."

"You're absolutely right." Greta turned to Winnie. "If I remember correctly, emergency procedures at the university called for covering a suspicious package."

"With a trash can or a piece of clothing," Winnie said. "Thanks for reminding me, Greta."

"The nearest trash can is in the coffee shop," Scarlett said.

Hal lugged the large, metal container from the shop, and tied a knot in the top of the plastic liner. Then he upended the can—liner and all—over the package. "A bit of improvisation," he said. "Garbage as makeshift insulation."

"Everyone outside, then, please, and away from the building," Winnie said. "Scarlett, will you call the police? I'm going to make sure no other staff are still on the premises."

"Don't be long," Scarlett said.

"I'll be right behind you."

Scarlett called 911 as she and the Barons rushed to the far end of the parking lot. She answered the dispatcher's questions, describing the size and location of the package. She stayed on the phone until the police arrived and Winnie was able to confirm the building was empty. Moments later, two officers with dogs headed inside while Winnie conferred with Officer Nina Garcia.

"We could probably head home at this point," Greta said. "They don't need extra people to worry about."

"Not yet," Hal said. "I need to know what's going on."

Scarlett smiled at the docent. Her employees felt every bit as protective of the museum's contents as she did.

"We can't leave, anyway." Greta pointed to police cars parked at either end of the block. "They've stopped traffic."

Scarlett was grateful for the extent of the police response and the proof that they were taking the museum's concerns seriously. Fascinated too, although she also had a sinking feeling about the evening's event. "Here come Winnie and Nina." Officer Garcia had become a friend. "Maybe they have good news."

Neither Winnie nor Nina wore a smile as they strode across the parking lot. The women were close in age and build, and both wore their dark hair in a ponytail. Winnie made her typical outfit of neat blue jeans, a tucked oxford shirt, and Converse sneakers appear as professional as Officer Garcia's Crescent Harbor Police uniform.

"You did the right thing by calling us," Nina said.

Scarlett felt unable to breathe for a moment. "Then it *is* a bomb?"

Nina held up a hand. "No. I should have been more clear. Calling us is always the right thing to do, just to be safe. But everything seems to be fine. Two detection dogs went in. One is trained for explosives, the other for drugs. Neither alerted to the package."

"Oh, thank heavens," Greta said.

Nina said, "The better news is that the officers and dogs are walking through the rest of the building. Purely as a precautionary measure."

She pointed to the radio at her shoulder. "Nothing reported so far, and you know what they say about no news."

"We considered the possibility of toxins too," Scarlett said. "Would the dogs alert to poison or something like anthrax? Winnie touched the package."

"We'll take it with us for further examination," Nina said, "but there's no visible powder, oily substance, or residue. We'll contact the post office too. In the meantime, if Winnie washes her hands thoroughly, that should be adequate."

Greta held up her phone. "I did a quick Internet search for Quartz Sutton, first in Larkfield, then in California as a whole."

"Any luck?" Nina asked.

"Not for Quartz, but I did find a Quinn Sutton in Larkfield. Shall I send that information to you?"

"Please. Does it include a phone number?"

"No."

"I bet the police have their ways of getting phone numbers," Hal said. "Am I right?"

"Oh yes." Nina's smile appeared. "We have our ways." The radio at her shoulder came to life as the officers in the museum declared the building clear. "That's it, then," Nina said. "While we have the package, we'll try to follow up on how it came to be here."

"Fantastic." Scarlett blew out a huge breath. "Thank you both, for being on your toes and taking care of this quickly."

When the police gave permission, the museum staff trooped back inside. Only the trash can standing in the middle of the lobby hinted that anything unusual had happened. As Hal returned it to the coffee shop, Greta's phone rang.

"What a nice surprise," Greta said, checking the display. "It's Henry Lang, Hal." She connected and greeted Henry warmly.

"A history pal of hers at Santa Rosa Junior College, north of San Francisco," Hal said. "We used to meet up with him at conferences."

"Henry, hold on a moment, will you?" Greta said. "Hal and a couple of friends are here. Do you mind if I put you on speakerphone? Wonderful." She tapped her phone, then held it up and gestured for the others to gather around. "Okay, Henry, could you repeat your question?"

"I need a favor," Henry said. "Well, it's more like a huge imposition. There's a surfing competition in Monterey that's making motel rooms impossible to get. So I'm wondering if you can put up a friend of mine overnight. He's a history buff. Nice fella. Coming your way to pick up antique mining equipment for the small museum where he volunteers. He's a bit down on his luck, but he'll more than repay you in stories. He's a terrific storyteller."

Greta was making a move-it-along motion toward the phone with her free hand. "His name, Henry," she said, finally breaking in. "Tell them his name."

"Quinn Sutton."

Three mouths dropped open. Scarlett could tell Greta enjoyed their reaction.

"We'd be happy to host him," Greta said to Hal's eager nodding.

"Henry," Hal cut in. "Does your old mining-enthusiast friend sometimes go by the name Quartz?"

Henry laughed. "He does. Do you know him?"

"No, but he sounds like someone we'll enjoy," Hal said. "When can we expect him?"

"I'm not sure. I'll have him give you a call."

"Did you send a package to Quartz here in Crescent Harbor?" Greta asked.

"No. Maybe he sent it to himself? Many, many thanks for this, my friends. The next time you come north, I'll treat you to dinner."

Greta disconnected. "I'd better update the police on the package." She dialed her phone and then asked to be connected with Chief Rodriguez. "Please tell them Greta Baron is calling about the suspicious package delivered to the Reed Museum this afternoon." While she waited to be connected, she pressed the button for speakerphone once more.

"Mrs. Baron, this is Chief Rodriguez. You have new information for us?"

"We've identified Quartz Sutton," Greta said, and she gave him the gist of Henry Lang's phone call.

"Very good," Rodriguez said. "When you see Mr. Sutton, please tell him that his package will be waiting for him here at the station."

"Here you go, lucky girl." Scarlett gave Cleo, her housemate and constant companion, a treat before she had to dash back to the museum.

The beautiful longhaired black cat purred and rubbed her forehead on the hem of Scarlett's trousers.

"Is that a thank-you? Or is it a promise to hit me up for another snack when I get home?" Scarlett decided Cleo's innocent blink meant "yes" to both questions.

The phone rang as she finished changing. "Uncanny timing," she said in response to Luke Anderson's warm greeting. "I just put on the moonstone necklace you gave me."

"Not uncanny at all," Luke said. "FBI training basically gives us ESP."

"Cool. So what am I thinking now?"

He didn't hesitate before saying, "You're glad the suspicious package didn't put the kibosh on your opening tonight."

"Wow, you're good. I almost believe in FBI ESP."

"Jokes aside," Luke said, "I'm glad it was a false alarm. How are you doing?"

"I'm fine. Hearing your voice has banished the last of the heebie-jeebies. Did you hear the rest of the story?" Scarlett told him about Quartz Sutton's impending visit.

"But the sender of the package remains anonymous? Curious," Luke said. "But curious things happen every day. I'm glad the opening is still on. See you there."

Scarlett rubbed Cleo between her ears. "Between you and me, the fewer curious things and unpleasant surprises, the better."

Soft jazz and merry voices met Scarlett's ears. She stood partway up the stairs to get a better view of the lobby full of happy museum supporters. The waitstaff carried trays of savory hors d'oeuvres, moving like well-choreographed dancers. Greta stood near the jazz trio, swaying to the music. Adding live music to the event had been the perfect touch. Scarlett waved to Greta then descended the stairs and performed her own dance, threading her way through the crowd to join Luke in the exhibit gallery. She found him with Hal and Winnie in front of Wyeth's painting of Long John Silver. Hal was bemoaning a missed opportunity for Greek to Me, the local theater group he belonged to.

"We should have coordinated with your exhibit," Hal said when he saw her. "We could have put on the musical version of *The Strange Case of Dr. Jekyll and Mr. Hyde*."

"Is that a thing?" Winnie asked.

"A fabulous thing." Hal pointed at Winnie. "You have a parrot, right?"

"Yes. Mac," Winnie said.

"Could you train Mac to say 'pieces of eight'?"

"Maybe," Winnie said. "How do you feel about actors who ad-lib, though? Because he might insist on winging it." She chuckled as Hal groaned over the pun. "I'll make another circuit in here, then head out to the lobby."

"Wouldn't it be fun to do *Treasure Island*? What do you think, Luke? Are you up for building a sailing ship?"

Luke, who often helped with set construction, saluted Hal. "Aye-aye, Cap'n."

"Sorry, I couldn't help overhearing." A young woman who'd been sitting on a bench studying the Wyeth pieces joined them. From her accent, Scarlett guessed she was Scottish. "A production of *Treasure Island* would be brilliant."

"As are you for saying so." Hal offered his hand. "Hal Baron. And these are my friends Luke Anderson and Scarlett McCormick, who is also our hostess this evening. She's the museum's head curator and responsible for mounting this exhibit. And here's my wife, Greta."

"A pleasure to meet all of you. I'm Tamsin Murchie. I'm a graduate student at the University of Edinburgh."

"Wonderful," Scarlett said. "Now we can brag that our opening had an international audience. What brings you all the way to Crescent Harbor?"

"Robert Louis Stevenson. He's my area of concentration. I'm researching his stay in California."

"Then if you haven't already met Maria Huerta, you must," Greta said.

"I haven't," Tamsin said.

"She's head of our historical society and an expert on area history. She's here somewhere this evening." Greta glanced around the room. When her phone began to buzz, she turned her attention to the chic, small bag slung over her shoulder. "Please excuse me."

Greta connected the call, but she only seemed able to slip occasional words into the conversation. "Yes, this is Greta. Ah, Mr. Sutton. Sorry, Quartz. It's a pleasure to hear— We're looking forward to— Yes— We're happy to have you."

Hal leaned his head closer in an effort to hear Quartz Sutton too.

"When can we exp—" Greta managed to fit in. After another moment or two she grabbed another chance. "Henry is indeed a good friend. When can we expect you? Well, that's— No, you won't be imposing. Not at all. And where are you now?"

Hal straightened, mouth gaping at the others. "Here," he whispered. "He's here, in the parking lot. Now."

"You're right, there is a 'do' at the museum tonight," Greta said.

"Is something going on?" Tamsin asked.

"Just the arrival of a houseguest," Scarlett said. "Somewhat unexpected."

"Hal." Luke caught him before he started listening in again. "To be clear, you didn't expect this guy this evening, right?"

"Not at all. It's a total surprise," Hal said.

"Would you like a suggestion?" Luke asked.

"Sure."

"Ask Greta to say you'll meet him outside. Make it by the museum sign at the entrance to the drive. There's plenty of light there, but it's away from the building and the vehicles in the parking lot."

"Do you really think that's necessary?" Hal asked.

"Not necessary, but a decent precaution," Luke said. "And as another, do you mind if I come along?"

"Not at all."

Scarlett tapped quickly on her own phone. "I'm texting Winnie. She and I will come too."

Seeing a concerned expression on Tamsin's face, Scarlett assured her there was nothing to worry about. She hoped she was right.

But as she and Winnie followed Luke and the Barons through the lobby toward the front door, Scarlett felt a prickle of unease run down her spine. She twisted around and made brief eye contact with someone watching her from the edge of the gallery door.

Rylla? She was wearing a different hat, but Scarlett was sure it was Rylla. How had she missed seeing her until now, and what was she doing here?

"Winnie, quick, in the gallery doorway. It's Rylla."

But when her friends peered in that direction, Scarlett had another surprise.

Rylla was nowhere in sight.

3

"You're sure it was Rylla?" Winnie asked. "She'd be hard to miss with that hair or the pink hat."

"I'm ninety-eight percent sure," Scarlett said. "She's wearing a different hat. Probably knitted. Close-fitting. Dark, but not black."

"Clothing?" Winnie asked.

"I didn't see anything but her head. She was peeking around the corner. Sorry."

"No problem. You go with the others. I'll see if I can find her. Just to talk, though. Keep it low-key."

"Right," Scarlett said. "It isn't worth making a big deal. There's no need to toss her out."

"Unless it turns out there is."

Hoping that need didn't arise, Scarlett hurried after the Barons and Luke. She hadn't told Winnie that Rylla had been watching them. She wasn't even fifty percent sure about that.

"Everything all right?" Luke asked.

"Quick change of plans. Winnie's checking on something. I think our mystery man's waiting for us."

"Speaking of plans," Hal said, "what's ours? If he passes muster, I can ride with him over to our place. That way Greta doesn't have to cut the evening short."

"If he passes muster, let's invite him to the opening," Scarlett said. "Does that pass muster with you?" She nudged Luke with her shoulder.

"I don't see why not." Luke nodded toward the museum's sign at the entrance to the drive. "Let's go meet him."

The sun had set, but the Reed's well-lit walkways gave Scarlett confidence.

Greta fell into step beside her, rubbing her upper arms. "I don't know if it's the fresh breeze or a frisson, but I'm suddenly chilly."

Hal took off his suit coat and slipped it around Greta's shoulders. "You can see the fellow's smile from here. Does that tell us anything?"

"Henry vouched for him," Greta said. "That tells us everything. I'll burrow into your coat and banish thoughts of frissons."

The man standing by the sign looked to be a few years older than Hal, putting him in his late sixties or early seventies. His clasped hands rested on a small but comfortable belly. A fluffy white beard might have hidden a less beaming smile. Bright eyes reflected the smile's warmth.

"A welcoming committee?" he said as they drew near. "If I'd known I'd get this kind of royal treatment, I might have gussied up." He gestured to his faded blue jeans, suspenders, boots, and brown flannel shirt. "At least I left my hat in the car. It's perfect for keeping the sun out of my eyes, but it has the air of a desperado."

Scarlett thought the rest of his outfit had an air of "ye olde prospector." That thought and his smile made her smile, and she relaxed. Then she wondered if she was being naive in letting her guard down.

"Quinn Sutton," their visitor said, nodding to each of them. "My enemies call me a quack and a fool. My students called me Mr. Sutton. My friends call me Quartz."

"Quartz," Greta said. "It's so good to meet you. I'm Greta." She introduced Hal, Scarlett, and Luke.

"Your nickname preceded you," Luke said, shaking Quartz's hand.

"Henry gave me away, did he? He's a kind rascal. If I'm lucky, he stuck to complimentary lies about me and hasn't made you regret your very kind invitation, Greta."

"He was most complimentary," Greta said.

"In that case, he was definitely lying. Isn't this an amazing bit of synchronicity, though?" Quartz asked. "Me showing up here at the museum, I mean, and finding you here too. Henry didn't know your address, but he told me you and Hal work here. I told him not to worry—if I could find the museum, then I could find you."

"I get a kick out of synchronicity," Hal said. "But we didn't learn your nickname from Henry. A package arrived here today, apparently addressed to you."

"Were you expecting it?" Luke asked. "You said something about having enemies."

"Enemies? An exaggeration. I hope." Quartz laughed, then added, "The package, yes. I was expecting it."

"The museum is an interesting choice for a mail drop, considering no one here knows you," Luke said.

"Well, when you only know one address in town, you make the most of it. So if by 'interesting' you mean 'unorthodox but ingenious,' then thank you." Quartz grinned. "Did it arrive safely?"

"I believe so," Scarlett said. "You can pick it up at the police station."

"At the police station?" Quartz put a hand to his heart. Even under the cool light cast by the streetlights and the museum's security lights, Scarlett thought his cheeks had grown pale above his beard. "What happened to it?"

"Your package is fine," Luke assured him. "So is the museum staff's training in how to respond to suspicious and possibly dangerous mail."

Quartz opened his mouth, but said nothing.

"The Crescent Harbor Police Department's bomb- and drug-sniffing dogs are beautifully trained too," Hal said.

Greta put a hand on Quartz's shoulder. "Are you all right?"

Quartz shook his head. "My enemies are right. I am a quack and fool. I'm ashamed of the trouble and alarm I must have caused. To whom should I apologize first and to whom most profusely?"

"I accept your apology on behalf of the museum," Scarlett said. "It wasn't all bad. It served as a reminder and a good drill. The police will be glad to know the full story too."

"In my rather weak defense, I had no idea the package would arrive before I did and before I had a chance to warn you of the imposition. Of the infringement." Quartz shook his head again. "I'm glad the package is safe with the police. I'll rescue it and apologize to them tomorrow."

"What do you think of joining us at our exhibit opening tonight?" Scarlett asked. "Art, music, hors d'oeuvres?"

"If you'll have an old fool, who lives too often in own his foolish world, then I'll be honored to join you."

Greta held Scarlett and Luke back with hands on their elbows. They watched Hal and Quartz strolling amiably toward the Reed's front door together, Hal throwing his head back in laughter at something the older man said.

"Do you have any reservations about him?" Greta asked Luke.

"I don't believe the man's actually a fool, and his story is plausible enough. So no, I have no reservations."

"Good, because I like him," Greta said. "Now for a more important question. If you don't have plans, will you join us for supper tomorrow night? Just the four of us, and really an excuse to eat dessert. I'm making a pear-and-fig tart with fresh fruit a former student dropped off the other day."

"I'm a pig for fresh figs," Luke said. "What do you think, Scarlett?"

"I'd love to," Scarlett said. She saw Winnie at the door, saying good night to a couple on their way out. "You two go on in," she said. "I want to hear what Winnie found out about another interesting situation." In response to Greta and Luke's raised eyebrows, she quickly added, "Nothing nearly as exciting as mysterious packages and strangers named Quartz. I'll tell you about it later."

Greta waved and disappeared into the murmur of conversation and music that wafted through the open door.

"Luke?" Scarlett said before he followed Greta. "I'm glad you were here and came out to meet Quartz with us."

He touched her cheek. "I am too. See you inside."

"The guy's a charmer," Winnie said after Luke walked away.

Scarlett gazed after Luke. "He is, isn't he?"

"We know Luke is," Winnie said. "I was talking about Quartz. When Hal introduced me as the head of security, Quartz fell all over himself apologizing for the trouble he'd caused. And do you know who else is charming this evening?"

"Do you want me to guess?"

"No, I'm dying to tell you. It's our friend Rylla. She is here, and she's here legitimately. She bought a membership this morning."

"Good for her," Scarlett said. "I'd like to know if that was before or after we found her in the gallery. Not that it matters, but then why make the crack about unwelcome riffraff?"

"Maybe she likes to play parts?" Winnie asked. "She wasn't easy to find in the crowd. She's wearing a skirt and sweater like something out of a 1930s Katharine Hepburn movie. Her hat matches the sweater. The clothes change her appearance almost completely."

"Except her eyes?"

"Except her eyes," Winnie agreed. "They're a stunning blue, aren't they? But somehow they strike me as . . . watchful? Wary? I'm not sure."

"I'm not sure either, but definitely recognizable." *And staring at me.*

Sizing me up? Guessing my next move? Scarlett told herself not to get carried away. "Thanks, Winnie."

Circulating through the lobby on her way to the gallery, Scarlett saw Greta and Tamsin talking to Maria Huerta. Maria's knowledge of local history would be an asset to Tamsin's research.

Luke met Scarlett in the gallery. He handed her a plate of mini mushroom tarts and promptly took one for himself.

"Thanks," Scarlett said. "The way to my heart is paved with tasty tidbits. And a turnout like this."

The gallery hummed with the conversations of people moving from picture to picture. Tamsin entered and cut straight across the room to stand before Wyeth's paintings for *Treasure Island*.

"Quartz is making his second tour of the room," Luke said. "Parrish and Wyeth might be his favorites. He's spent most of his time with them, especially the pieces featuring Long John Silver." He took another tart and popped it in his mouth.

"How about you?" Scarlett asked. "Do you have a favorite?"

"I just gave my favorite a plate of tasty treats."

"Then ate most of them."

"Oops. I can fix that," Luke said. "Wait here."

"I'll wait over there with Long John Silver. I see a couple of people I want to say hi to."

Rylla, in her retro-chic outfit, had joined Tamsin at the Wyeths, and the two were chatting.

"Rylla, Tamsin, hello," Scarlett said. "I didn't know you two knew each other."

"We don't," Rylla said. "You've interrupted our polite introductory small talk. She says she's into Stevenson, so I was about to spout what he said about the landscape around here: 'The greatest meeting of land and sea in the world.'"

"That's beautiful," Scarlett said.

"But not Stevenson," Tamsin said. "Sorry to be blunt, but he is my area of expertise."

"You introduced yourself as a graduate student," Rylla said. "How does that make you an expert?"

"I didn't mean to sound so full of myself," Tamsin said. "But I do know the quotation is from Francis McComas, not Stevenson. McComas was an Australian painter. Born in Tasmania, actually."

"I've seen it attributed to Stevenson over and over," Rylla argued.

"It's lovely no matter who said it," Tamsin placated. "And often misattributed, so you can hardly be blamed for following along. If you're interested, though, the museum has two McComas paintings. Nice meeting you."

Rylla's lips pressed together in an unhappy slash as her cheeks flushed.

Scarlett watched Tamsin walk away. The flash of a smile she caught on the Scotswoman's face made her wonder: *Did Tamsin needle Rylla on purpose?*

Saturday evening, Scarlett and Luke walked over to Greta and Hal's for their dinner date. The Barons lived near downtown Crescent Harbor, in an area popular with strolling tourists who daydreamed about living in the cozy houses they passed.

"Come in," Hal said. "The curtain is about to rise on Greta's delectable vegetable soup, and the audience will be on its feet for the fresh fig-and-pear tart." He peered past them down the front walk and his eyebrows rose.

"Excellent," said an approaching voice. "I'm as ravenous as an old raccoon."

"Quartz, how wonderful!" Hal said with increased volume. "All three guests right on time."

Scarlett and Luke passed confused grins, but didn't question Hal's loud announcement.

Stepping inside, Scarlett saw a startled Greta motion to her from the kitchen doorway.

"I didn't know he was going to be here," Greta whispered, handing Scarlett a stack of plates. "We thought he left when he said goodbye after breakfast."

With sudden understanding that Hal's announcement had been a warning to his wife, Scarlett offered Greta a sympathetic smile before taking the plates to the table.

Though unexpected, Quartz was an entertaining addition to the supper table. He held them spellbound with a centuries-old tale of a ship that navigated into the Salton Sea from the Gulf of California, went aground with its treasure of black pearls, and disappeared into the sands of time when the sea dried up.

"You make it sound entirely plausible," Greta said. "Has anyone found primary source material backing up these stories? Diaries or letters?"

"I'm as much a nut for old diaries as I am for mining equipment," Quartz said. "I don't know whether it's more sad or enticing that I've only uncovered a few newspaper accounts and they're mostly tales of old tales."

"I enjoy that kind of 'history,'" Greta said. "Tales tell us something about the eras in which they arise."

"Yes, indeed." Quartz finished his soup and wiped the bowl with a piece of bread.

"How do these tales of a ship lost in the desert connect to your interest in mines?" Luke asked.

"I can't say they do. Not unless other stories about caches of black pearls found in abandoned mines are true."

"Do you believe the stories?" Hal asked.

"If they aren't true, then they're a lovely fiction," Greta said.

Quartz gave an amiable shrug. "And fiction is often the best treasure of all."

"Did you have any trouble reclaiming your package at the police station?" Luke asked.

"Reclaiming my own treasure? None at all."

Scarlett sensed an opening for another story. "Is your treasure a secret?"

"You're curious?" Quartz asked.

"Always," Scarlett admitted.

"Then you're in good company," Quartz said. "May you never lose that skill. It is a skill, when used properly. No, my treasure isn't a secret, but I won't tell you what it is."

"Doesn't that make it a secret?" Luke asked.

"I might be splitting hairs," Quartz said. "See what you think. My treasure isn't a secret, but I am secretive."

Luke nodded. "Beautifully split."

"Thank you. Secretive I might be, but I am not without my redeeming qualities. I've given you several clues as to the nature of my treasure and will continue to do so throughout my stay."

Greta and Hal widened their eyes.

"What if there isn't enough time to decipher your clues?" Greta asked.

"Ah, kind hostess," Quartz said. "Given enough time, I believe you will prevail. If not, and with good luck, it won't matter." Eyes gleaming, he leaned across the table toward Greta. "In the end, all will be revealed."

4

Sunday, after church, Scarlett chuckled over a story about a prizewinning custard pie recipe in the *Rip Current News*. "Sounds like someone has egg on their face, Cleo. The recipe came from the Internet, not from the cook's old granny. Good old *Rip Current*. All the news and gossip fit to print." She shook the paper into order and refolded it.

Cleo, in the middle of tidying her black fur, stopped to give Scarlett a feline scowl.

"Please forgive me for disturbing you, your majesty," Scarlett apologized.

Cleo blinked and returned to her work, extending one elegant back leg.

"My laundry needs doing too. Any chance you'll do it for me while I'm at the farmers market this afternoon?"

Cleo stretched both back legs until they shivered. Then she flopped on her side and gazed at Scarlett upside down.

"That's sort of the way I feel about laundry too." Scarlett glanced out the window. "It's a gorgeous day for the market. I'm sorry you can't come along." Cleo enjoyed getting outside, but Scarlett limited her to the back deck and occasional excursions.

Scarlett laid the paper on the sofa, knowing that Cleo would see it as the most irresistible place for a Sunday afternoon nap. Sure enough, in the time it took Scarlett to slip on her shoes and collect her market basket and sun hat, Cleo had discovered the paper. As Scarlett let herself out the door, Cleo heaved a luxurious cat sigh and curled herself into a dream.

With the day so beautiful, Scarlett walked to the pedestrian mall in the center of Crescent Harbor. Luke had said he would meet her there if he didn't get called to the office in San Francisco. Potential last-minute changes to any plans they made was a price to pay for dating an FBI agent, but Luke was worth it. He was an honorable man who kept his promises.

He was waiting for her on the corner at the market's entrance, wearing a backpack to hold his own purchases. "Would you like me to take your basket?"

"No, but thank you. Unless I go crazy over the memory of Greta's tart and buy twenty-five pounds of pears and fresh figs."

"It was pretty spectacular."

"Quartz liked it. He had two pieces," Scarlett said. "I considered that myself, but I managed to refrain."

"You could have, you know. Greta offered."

"I know, but that would have left Greta and Hal with one left over. I couldn't bear the thought that one of them would have to be a martyr watching the other eat that last, luscious slice for a bedtime snack. Or worse—what if neither of them agreed to be the martyr and there was bloodshed, all because of my greedy decision to have a second piece? How could I live with myself? Would you buy fresh arugula at the farmers market with a person like that?"

"All of that ran through your mind when Greta looked at you and said the single word, 'another'?"

"More or less."

"You are second only to Quartz with your gift for tall tales," Luke said.

"Thanks. His lost ship of the desert is a doozy."

"With enough believable details to make the whole thing almost plausible," Luke said.

They strolled on, and somewhere between a stand selling early pumpkins and one with peppers and tomatoes, Luke tucked Scarlett's arm in his. "Hal and Greta are a terrific couple. Perfectly in tune with each other."

"They are."

"So don't you think they could have split the last piece of tart between them if you'd eaten the other one?"

"Split it? What an abhorrent idea. Fair warning, Luke, don't ever try to come between me and a full slice of—well, almost anything."

"Yes, ma'am." Luke laughed. "Thank goodness you've revealed your true nature. If you ever want my slice of something along with yours, give the word. I won't stand between it and you."

"Wise man. For your sake, though, I'll try to control myself."

"Speaking of revealing, I wonder if Quartz has revealed how long he's planning to stay," Luke said. "Isn't that him talking to the guy at the avocado stand?"

"He's still here? Wow. If he hasn't dropped a clue about how long he's staying, Hal and Greta should ask him."

"The man who came to stay," Luke mused. "I bet there's a tall tale along those lines. Shall we go ask him?"

"Yes, and let's listen for clues about his package. The puzzle bug's bitten me. If he's going to reveal all, I'd love to figure out what was in the package before the revelation."

"His clues might not be any better than some of those tips we get at the agency," Luke warned.

"But we don't have a chance of putting clues together unless we hear them," Scarlett said.

"You are excellent FBI material."

"Thank you. I'm a decent cook too. After we talk to Quartz, I'll pick up some avocados. Play your cards right, and I'll make avocado soup with shrimp for you."

Quartz had left the avocado stand to look over a display of leather goods. He returned their greeting with obvious delight. "Wasn't that a lovely time last night? And doesn't this artisan do fine work? Makes all of these belts and wallets and such himself."

Scarlett breathed in the smell of fine leather. "They're beautiful."

Quartz stroked the cover of a tooled leather book. "And these journals—any writer or diarist would be proud to put pen to paper in one of them. Think of the stories and secrets they'll each hold someday." He traced a leaf design down the spine of a journal, then stuck his hands in the pockets of his worn jeans. "Where to next? I'll come along."

"Avocados, if you don't mind backtracking," Luke said.

"Not a bit. I'm not in the market for anything, except maybe a bouquet of flowers for Greta's table."

The three of them returned to the avocado stand.

"I enjoy watching people make their choices," Quartz said as Scarlett picked up one avocado, then another. "How they settle on the exact fruits and vegetables that appeal to them most. As carefully chosen as the words of a writer like Robert Louis Stevenson, or so I imagine."

"You're a Stevenson fan?" Luke asked.

"It's hard not to be," Quartz said. "First-rate adventure stories. Did you know that half of his original manuscripts are missing?"

"Lost, like the ship in the desert." Scarlett paid for her avocados, and the men trailed her around the corner to a baker's stall, where she picked out a loaf of sourdough rye. "Will you be in town long, Quartz? There's a scholar in the area who's researching the time Stevenson spent in California. I can introduce you, if you'd like."

Quartz appeared to consider the offer, then shook his head. "A young woman from Scotland? I met her at your opening. I'm sure she's knowledgeable, but I'm a solitary codger. Much like the prospectors of old who preferred keeping their own company with their own ends in mind."

Except when it comes to walking around a farmers market, Scarlett thought. She caught Luke's amused eye and felt certain the same thought had occurred to him. Further proof of his ESP.

"Were you able to make your connection and pick up the mining equipment you came to get?" Luke asked.

"Yes sirree," Quartz said. "And with a bonus. The fella gave me another lead."

"Is there really that much old mining equipment to be had around here?" Luke asked.

Quartz touched a finger to his nose. "I didn't say that."

"Do your leads always pan out?" Scarlett asked.

"No, but I love the hunt."

"But you won't say more?" Luke asked.

"Before the hunt, it's time for stealth. After the hunt, there's time for regaling, for burnishing—"

"For embellishing?" Luke asked.

"Of course," Quartz said. "The story of the hunt becomes the stuff of legends. Depending on the outcome."

"It isn't just the hunt you love," Scarlett said. "You love stories too."

Quartz gazed off into the distance. "Think of all the stories out there that we've never heard. Enough lost stories to fill the hold of the lost ship of the desert a hundred times over. Stories are the islands in the storms of our lives."

"You're a philosopher as well as an enthusiast of antique mining equipment," Luke said.

"I defy anyone to teach high school for forty years without becoming a philosopher of one kind or another. What's next on our shopping list?"

"Fruit," Scarlett said. "Pears."

"Ah, and figs?" Quartz asked. "Greta's tart hit the spot, didn't it? She practically insisted that I have the last slice as a bedtime snack. Halfway down this row, on the right, you'll find your pears. Figs in the next row over. And if you'll take a suggestion, a dollop of fresh goat cheese would be a superb addition."

"Oh." Scarlett put a hand to her heart. "Goat cheese. Yes. You are a man of many talents, Quartz."

"I leave you now, with a most sincere bow of thanks for that compliment and a word of caution. The islands I spoke of?"

"The islands that are made up from the stories of our lives, giving us shelter from the storms?" Scarlett asked.

"You'll be wise to remember that not every island is a safe port."

Quartz bade them a good afternoon, and Scarlett and Luke watched him walk back the way they'd come.

"On to the pears and figs?" Luke asked.

"He had three pieces of the tart," Scarlett said with a sigh.

Luke tucked her arm in his again. "Is that envy I hear?"

She grinned at him. "Maybe a little."

Scarlett enjoyed the variety of people at the farmers market every bit as much as the variety of fresh produce and other goods. She also enjoyed the feeling of being at home in Crescent Harbor and seeing so many people she knew. As she and Luke passed stands selling squash and melons, they exchanged greetings with the police chief, Gabriel Rodriguez, and his wife, Maddie. The chief held a market basket loaded with artichokes, to which Maddie was adding okra as she scolded him for wrinkling his nose. Farther along, they heard Danielle Jenson, owner of the Vintage Idiot antique shop, haggling over the price for a bushel of nectarines.

"The idea of the story itself might be one of Quartz's clues," Luke said.

"Stories in general or lost stories," Scarlett said. "He's big on lost and missing things too."

Scarlett bought a dozen pears so she would have enough after the tart to add to her lunches throughout the week. When they moved on to the fig stand, they encountered Tamsin.

"How do you like our market?" Luke asked.

"It reminds me of the lovely market below the castle in Edinburgh," Tamsin said. "It comes as a nice surprise, as well. I rather thought Americans bought all their food shrouded in packaging from huge supermarkets."

"There's always that option." Scarlett didn't know Tamsin well enough to trust her ears, but she thought she'd detected the same snip in Tamsin's voice that she'd heard directed at Rylla Friday evening.

"I'll get the figs," Luke said. "Then I'll take what we've got so far to the car and catch up with you."

"Sounds good. Thanks." Scarlett watched Tamsin studying a fig and decided to give her the benefit of the doubt. *She's young and a stranger in a strange land.* Scarlett knew what that felt like from personal experience. Besides, she liked Tamsin's open, friendly face. "I saw you and Greta talking to our town librarian, Maria Huerta, Friday night. Will she be able to help with your research?"

"Aye. She gave me the name of a woman who's meant to be here today. I thought I'd track her down. I've got her name." Tamsin took a small notebook from her messenger bag.

Scarlett immediately had notebook envy. She'd used one like Tamsin's for her fieldwork and when she traveled. Tamsin slipped an elastic band from around the smooth, leather cover and leafed through the pages. Scarlett felt the urge to peer over her shoulder to see what sort of notes she kept, what kind of story her notes told. *As if I'm channeling Quartz.*

"Here it is," Tamsin said. "Sophie Morata from Left Field Farm. Maria said Sophie might be able to help me follow the trail of Robert Louis Stevenson's ill-fated and nearly fatal solo camping trip in September 1879." Tamsin shuddered. "'Ill-fated and nearly fatal.' Not descriptions I'd like attached to my travels."

"No kidding. I've never heard that story, but I can introduce you to Sophie. She sells goat cheese, honey, and heirloom apples, and I happen to want some goat cheese."

On their way to the Left Field Farm stand, Scarlett told Tamsin the little she knew about Sophie. "She's in her early sixties, lean, and fit. She could be the poster girl for an organic farmers association. Or rather, the poster lady."

"And she's still helping out on a farm at sixty?" Tamsin asked.

"She owns the farm."

Scarlett and Tamsin stood back while Sophie attended to a line of customers. Sophie, with a gray braid down her back and a wide-brimmed hat shading her face, had a smile for each customer. The line dwindled, and Sophie turned her smile to Scarlett and Tamsin.

Scarlett bought her goat cheese, then introduced Tamsin. "She's a graduate student studying Robert Louis Stevenson, and Maria Huerta mentioned you might be able to give her some information."

"I know he took a camping trip in this area," Tamsin said. "Do you know anything about that? And I'd love to visit your farm if that's all right."

Sophie's smile disappeared. "You're the second person today who's asked about my property and what I know."

"About Stevenson?" Tamsin asked.

"No." Sophie didn't elaborate. She assessed Tamsin silently for a moment. "You're welcome to visit the farm Tuesday afternoon if you'd like."

"Would you like me to give you a ride, Tamsin?" Scarlett asked.

"That would be brilliant," Tamsin replied.

"Please remember it's a working farm, though," Sophie said. "If you come, don't expect to wander around."

"Oh, no worries," Tamsin said. "I'm much more interested in finding the creek where Stevenson camped than getting in your way."

"It isn't just a question of getting in my way," Sophie said. "It's a question of getting into trouble—or very real danger."

5

"Sometimes I like to live dangerously," Scarlett said as she and Luke took a walk Monday evening. "Care to join me?"

"An interesting invitation. What do you have in mind?"

"Fish tacos at The Salty Dog."

A worry line appeared between Luke's eyebrows. "Did they fail a health inspection or something?"

"No, but Cleo will be royally affronted when I come home smelling of fish I didn't share with her from a place named for a dog." Scarlett tsked. "I'll have to make it up to her with extra chin rubs."

"Or you can have salad and not mention dogs," Luke offered.

"Hmm, no. I really do want fish tacos, and I like to keep our relationship honest."

"Are cats honest?" Luke raised an eyebrow in doubt. "Seems to me they're fairly secretive. Sneaky, even."

"In other words, somewhat human? But cats don't pretend to be anything but what they are, which includes secretive, sneaky, indifferent, and adorable. Ask them about it, and they'll flick their tails and stare at you like 'whatever.'"

"This is why you're good at solving mysteries," Luke said. "You're a solid judge of character. Feline as well as human."

Their discussion had carried them to The Salty Dog. Luke held the door for Scarlett. Despite the crowd, they didn't have to wait long before the hostess led them to a table with an ocean view. On their way, Scarlett spotted Greta, Hal, and Quartz at a small corner table on the other side of the room. Hal waved them over.

"You go and say hi for me," Luke said, waving back. "I'll hold our table."

"Okay, be right back."

Quartz beamed up at Scarlett when she reached their table. "This is what I love about Crescent Harbor—the sophistication of world-class museums, dining, and scenery while also providing the intimacy of a cozy small town. Nice to see you again, Scarlett."

"I couldn't have sung Crescent Harbor's praises better myself," Scarlett said. "Nice to see the three of you again so soon."

"Quartz is treating us to an evening out," Hal said.

"It's the least I can do, considering all they're doing for me."

"He also told us that someday he wants to find a display similar to our *Art from the Golden Age of Illustration* exhibit," Greta said, "but this one detailing the golden age of British short stories."

"Interesting idea," Scarlett said. "A display with original manuscripts?"

"The first drafts of famous writers," Quartz said. "Wouldn't that be fascinating?"

"Even more fascinating," Greta said, "is adding that tidbit about what fascinates Quartz to our collection of possible clues. I'm determined to figure out what arrived in his package before he reveals all."

Quartz laughed, gazing proudly at Greta.

Probably the way he smiled when a brilliant student pleased him back when he was a teacher, Scarlett thought. She wished the trio a good evening and rejoined Luke.

"Check out the menu," Luke said.

"No need. My heart is set on fish tacos."

"And I already ordered them for you. But I wanted you to see the logo—the scruffy dog in a sea captain's hat. Remind you of anyone?"

Scarlett chuckled. "Our friend Quartz?"

"The man who came to stay. I guess calling him scruffy is kind of rude, though."

"There's nothing necessarily wrong with scruffy," Scarlett said. "Some people cultivate the look."

"And pay big bucks for it," Luke said. "I've done it a few times for undercover work."

"Do you pull it off? I mean, convincingly? No, forget I asked. Of course you do. Speaking of the man who came to stay, he's treating Greta and Hal tonight."

"Nice of him," Luke said. "Although it also seems like the least he could do."

"Exactly what he said. Then he added, 'considering all they're doing for me.' Not all they've done. All they're doing, present tense."

"I admire Hal and Greta's unflappable equanimity," Luke said.

Their food arrived in red baskets—three fish tacos each with crispy onion rings on the side.

Scarlett devoured her first taco before a question occurred to her. "Are you getting any vibes about Quartz?" she asked. "Could he be one of those guys who isn't on the up and up? A grifter?"

"Anything's possible," Luke said. "Vibes aren't really part of my skill set. I'm more of a facts kind of guy."

"And the facts are that Greta's professor friend Henry vouched for Quartz, and here he is treating them to supper out. That's not really con man behavior, is it?" Scarlett reasoned.

"And here he comes in person. Nice to see you again, Quartz." Luke offered Quartz a chair.

Quartz sat, flagged a waiter, and asked for a cup of coffee.

"Have you had a chance to follow up on your new lead?" Scarlett asked.

"A dead end."

"I'm sorry." Scarlett knew how frustrating that could be.

"I would sigh and drown my sorrows," Quartz said, accepting the coffee the waiter brought him. He gulped some before continuing. "But drowning sorrows is no way to go through life. Besides, I have another lead. I've heard of an abandoned quicksilver mine. I plan to check it out tomorrow."

"Quick as opposed to slow silver?" Luke asked.

"*Argentum vivum*," Quartz said. "Living silver."

"Mercury," Scarlett said.

"Absolutely right," Quartz said. "Quicksilver is the more poetic name used for mercury."

"I hope you don't plan to go into this abandoned mine," Luke said.

"Quicksilver, used as an adjective, suggests sudden and rapid changes in mood," Quartz said. "The conditions in old mines can change suddenly and rapidly too. Old mines are no place for old men. Or anybody."

"Not to mention the toxicity of mercury," Luke said.

"Toxic, yes, but not magnetic. Unlike the most powerful magnet of all—true love."

"That's a sudden and rapid change of direction," Scarlett said.

"Not entirely," Quartz said. "I was drawn here to Crescent Harbor by my love for old mining equipment. I'm an absolute sucker for forged metal and rust."

"Stories and philosophy too," Scarlett said.

"You bet. I believe I said something about loving the life of a solitary old codger too. But I'm never truly alone. I have my rust, my stories, and my philosophizing. My diary too. Words are good company." Quartz finished his coffee and stood. "I'm off for a walk along the beach and to let my gracious hosts have time to themselves."

The moment Quartz was out the door, Greta and Hal came over to the table.

"How's the guest?" Scarlett asked.

"Nice and undeniably entertaining, but we're looking forward to no extra voice in the house," Greta said. "As interesting as the topics are, it's amazing how wearing a single voice can be."

"Watching the news alone will be a luxury," Hal said.

"Have you asked when he's leaving?" Luke asked.

"We have, and we've received an answer." Hal scratched his head in an uncanny imitation of Quartz. "And that answer is that he can't be sure."

"We don't expect him to stay much longer," Greta said. "This really did seem like a farewell dinner, don't you think, Hal?"

"I hate to tempt the fates with an answer to that," Hal said. "But whether or not it was, we should skedaddle before our guest returns to the house. See you at the museum tomorrow, Scarlett." The Barons waved and strolled away.

Scarlett offered the last of her onion rings to Luke. "Thanks," she said when he took them. "I'll explode if I eat another bite."

"Talk about living dangerously."

"It wouldn't be pretty, that's for sure. Speaking of living dangerously, do you know Sophic Morata?"

"No, why?"

"I can't forget what she said about visiting Left Field Farm. What do you suppose she meant when she said there's 'very real danger'?"

"Farms can be dangerous," Luke said.

"I know that."

"Equipment, machinery, large animals." Luke ticked off on his fingers. "Chemicals."

"Left Field is organic."

"Organic doesn't mean nontoxic," Luke said. "Organic pesticides do kill insects."

"Huh. You're right."

"She can't have people showing up expecting a tour. Or showing up expecting to wander around idyllic pastures and orchards like some of the illustrations in the exhibit."

"Especially Jessie Willcox Smith's work," Scarlett said. "I love her stuff, but it's highly romanticized. A young woman I know calls Smith's art spun sugar."

"That might be a bit harsh," Luke said.

"But pure Rylla. She's sure of herself, has definite opinions, and a style that's pretty far from spun sugar. Oh, another potential danger is Sophie's honeybees. She's probably not allergic to stings, but that's another reason not to have people wandering around."

"Yet," Luke said.

"What?"

"Sophie isn't allergic yet. An allergy to bee venom can develop. A person can be fine one sting, and then 'hello, anaphylactic shock' the next."

Scarlett shivered. "Call me paranoid, but suddenly I'm not sure this trip is a good idea after all."

The following morning, Scarlett set the newspaper aside after breakfast, grabbed a pen and a notepad, and plopped down on the sofa.

Cleo joined her, landing gracefully in her lap.

"Good. I can use your help, Cleo. I'm making a list of possible clues to what might be in Quartz's package. We have fifteen minutes, then I'm off to work."

Cleo butted her head against Scarlett's pen.

"It is kind of like butting our heads against a wall." Scarlett rubbed the cat between her ears. "I hardly know him. You don't know him at all. And despite everything he's said, he hasn't revealed much of anything that sounds like a clue to me."

Cleo purred, the pink tip of her tongue showing.

"Yes, you are a lovely girl, and you love hearing me think out loud, don't you? I could outline the most evil plan in the world, and you wouldn't mind as long as I sounded like I was purring."

Cleo stretched the toes of one front paw and then rested it on Scarlett's wrist.

"Thanks for the paw of confidence. Okay, here's what I do know. Quartz is a nice guy who likes stories." Scarlett jotted *stories*. She reflected for a moment, then wrote, *philosophy, old mining equipment, rust, treasure—lost and otherwise*. "He's talked about a lost ship in the desert and abandoned mines. He's staying longer than anyone expected, but that's either miscommunication or eccentricity, neither of which would be a clue. He describes himself as a loner. That makes him sound like a cat."

Cleo sat up with her ears swiveling.

"And my list sounds like drivel." Scarlett tore the paper from the pad, crumpled it into a ball, and tossed it on the floor. Cleo flew after the paper.

While the cat batted it from one end of the living room to the other, Scarlett batted around the idea of rewriting her list in one of her old field notebooks. She'd envied Tamsin's. Maybe finding and using her own would give her the inspiration she needed.

She and Tamsin planned to drive out to Left Field Farm after lunch. Rather than hunting for her old notebooks, Scarlett found herself pondering whether she and Tamsin would manage to stay out of whatever danger waited for them there.

Scarlett made a beeline for the museum coffee shop when she arrived at the Reed, sighing with relief when Allie put a cup of coffee in her hand. She inhaled the coffee steam, then took a careful sip and thanked her best friend.

"So how were the fish tacos at The Salty Dog last night?" Allie asked.

"Were you there? Why didn't you come say hi?"

"I wasn't there. I ran into your new social secretary, Quartz. He told me."

"When did you meet him? You weren't at the opening Friday night."

"He came in for a while yesterday," Allie said. "Nice guy. Chatty."

"You've noticed that?" Scarlett laughed. "What else did you talk about?"

"Jellyfish, sea otters, and the odds of being attacked by a shark while swimming, surfing, or boating. Treating Greta and Hal to dinner out. And what you had on your fish tacos."

"Wow. Anything else?"

"Let's see." Allie drummed her fingertips on her chin. "He'd love to see a manatee in real life. His favorite kind of stone is the fossilized coral called Petoskey stone, and his wife was a saint who put up with his nonsense. He misses her a lot."

"A wide-ranging conversation."

"The kind I always have time for."

Scarlett smiled at her friend. "You're a good soul, Allie. He seems kind of lonely."

"'Lonely' sounds more accurate than 'bona fide loner.' That's what he called himself, but the man surely loves an audience. I almost expect him to wander in here today and attach himself to a tour group. Or a family that needs an old hound dog."

"He is kind of like a friendly mutt, isn't he?"

"What's his story?" Allie asked.

"Good question. When I have an answer, I'll let you know."

Scarlett went upstairs to her office, where the coffee powered her through emails and the first draft of her monthly report for the board.

When she emptied the first cup, she took a stroll through the first-floor exhibits, finishing in the *Art from the Golden Age of Illustration* exhibit. Rylla was there with her drawing pad. Before Scarlett had a chance to greet her, Greta arrived with no sign of her usual smile. She stopped just inside the door and waved Scarlett over.

"Hal will be late this morning," Greta said. "Unfortunately, that means we'll be short one docent for the first tour."

"Don't worry about the tour. Is he all right?"

Worry creased two lines between her eyebrows. "He's all right. He's talking to the police."

"What happened?" Scarlett asked. "If you need to be with him, don't worry about the tours. We'll make do."

Greta waved the suggestion away. "We don't exactly know what's happened. It's Quartz. His truck is still parked at our house, and his clothes and toiletries are in the guest room. He told us he would make his specialty muffins for breakfast this morning, and he bought the ingredients, but we haven't seen him since he left The Salty Dog. As far as we can tell, he didn't make it to our house last night."

"You tried calling his phone, of course."

"It rings and rings, and then we get a message saying the subscriber can't be found." Greta rubbed her hands as if they were suddenly cold. "Quartz is missing."

6

Scarlett put her arm around Greta's shoulders and guided her to a bench along the gallery wall. "What's the law enforcement procedure in California to report that someone is missing?" she asked. "Luke's in San Francisco today, or I'd call and ask him. But is there a waiting period before police get involved?"

"I've been worried about that," Greta said. "That Quartz won't be considered missing yet because it hasn't been long enough. But we know how good and responsive our Crescent Harbor police are. They've already checked with area hospitals to rule out accident or sudden illness."

"Okay, that's good. Do you know anything specific about where Quartz was headed on his walk last night?"

"I don't even know anything general. He just said that he felt like a stroll."

"Well, he told Luke and me that he was going for a walk on the beach."

Greta pulled out her phone. "I'll let Hal know." Greta's call found Hal still at the police station. The worry lines between her eyebrows didn't disappear during the quick exchange of information.

"Any news?" Scarlett asked when Greta took the phone from her ear.

"No. Hal gave them Henry's phone number in case he can be of any help."

"That's good."

"And they recommended we change our locks," Greta said. "Quartz had our spare house key on him."

"Will you do it?"

"I think we have to."

Scarlett suddenly recalled another conversation earlier in the day. "Allie saw him after he left The Salty Dog. It sounded like he had a lot to say."

"He usually does."

"Maybe he mentioned something useful to her," Scarlett said. "Are you keeping the disappearance quiet for now?"

"I don't know why we should, but I've never dealt with anything like this. And in case you can't tell, I'm feeling deeply flustered."

"I can tell," Scarlett said.

"Time to put a stop to that." Greta stood up. "Being flustered won't help anyone. That said, it seems counterproductive to keep this hush-hush. If Quartz disappeared with serious health issues or dementia, the police wouldn't hesitate to issue an alert."

"BOLO," Scarlett said, getting up too. "Be on the lookout."

"That's it. You see? I do some of my best thinking on my feet, and now I don't sound flustered at all."

"You sound like the clear-thinking, efficient Greta I've come to know and admire."

Greta squeezed Scarlett's hand. "I hope—no, I *pray* that Hal and I are blowing this out of proportion. That Quartz shows up at noon, asks what's for lunch, and has another long-winded story to tell us."

Scarlett nodded toward Rylla, who was packing her art materials into her backpack. She slung the pack on one shoulder and started toward the door.

"Nice to see you again, Rylla," Scarlett said.

Rylla said something indistinct as she brushed past without slowing or making eye contact.

"What did she say?" Greta asked. "She scuttled by so quickly I missed it."

"That she remembered an appointment? Or maybe she said something about enjoyment." Scarlett shrugged and tried to remember if she had noticed Rylla wearing earbuds while she drew. *But we already decided it doesn't matter if people know Quartz is missing*, she thought. *Or that it probably doesn't.*

"Let's go find out what Allie can tell us," Greta said. "I'll buy you a cup of coffee. It's been a rough morning, and you did a great job of listening and then talking me back into a place of calm."

Allie waved as they approached the coffee shop. When they were close enough, she quietly asked, "Did you tell Rylla to leave?"

Scarlett stopped short. "Did she say that?"

"No. I guessed based on the way she beetled out of here with her head down. She struck me as a cross between a scolded puppy and someone with places to go and things to do. Coffee?"

"Two, please," Greta said. "And, if you have time, a recap of your conversation with Quartz last night. We're afraid he's gone missing."

"Well, that's no good." Allie closed her eyes for several seconds, clearly organizing her thoughts. "He said he'd just left you at The Salty Dog and he was going for a walk on the beach." She prepared coffees and handed them to Scarlett and Greta. "He asked what kinds of critters I come across, dangerous or otherwise, when I surf."

"Did he say anything about other plans for the evening?" Greta asked.

"No. He said a lot, but nothing about plans. And I didn't ask. I enjoyed talking to him, but I hadn't had supper, so I didn't prolong the chat with questions. Now I'm sorry for that."

"He might not have told you if you had," Greta said. "He enjoys being mysterious."

"Or you might still be there listening," Scarlett said, then winced.

"That was uncalled for. Greta, did he tell you about the lead he got on an abandoned quicksilver mine?"

"He did, but he said he'd never go into an old mine alone."

"He told us that too," Scarlett said. "But what if he went with whoever gave him the lead?"

"If he did," Allie said, "maybe they wanted an early start and Quartz spent the night with the guy."

The worry line appeared between Greta's eyebrows again. "He gets as excited about old mining equipment as my grandson does about new knock-knock jokes. Taking off at daybreak to find a mine could be more exciting than making muffins."

"Wouldn't he let you know?" Scarlett asked. "Call so you wouldn't worry?"

"I'm not sure," Greta said. "Except for staying longer than we expected, he's been incredibly considerate, but I don't know him well enough to say for sure what he would or wouldn't do."

"But if he gets as excited as a kid, maybe like a kid, it's possible he forgot to call," Allie said. "You don't know who gave him the lead?"

Greta pulled out her phone. "No, but now we have a lead ourselves. Thank you, Allie. I'll call Hal."

That afternoon, Scarlett and Tamsin made their trip to see Sophie Morata. The half-hour drive to Left Field Farm took them along a winding highway east, away from the coast.

"Do you think we'll see redwoods on the farm?" Tamsin asked. "I've only seen them in passing, and I'd love to see them up close. I've read there are groves of them in a regional park near Ms. Morata's farm. If there are any actually on the farm, I want to get photos.

Just think, Stevenson would have marveled at the very same trees."

The young Scotswoman's enthusiasm brought Quartz to Scarlett's mind. She'd heard no updates from Greta or Hal.

"I was pleased to see works by Florence Harrison and Helen Stratton in your illustrator's exhibit," Tamsin said, bubbling over a new topic.

Scarlett glanced at Tamsin, but before she could say a word, the younger woman started rambling about the mystery behind who Florence really was—Emma Florence Harrison, who studied at the Glasgow School of Art, or Florence Susan Harrison from Australia.

They turned off the highway onto Left Field Farm's private road, passing apple and pear orchards on one side and fenced pastureland with goats on the other. The road ended between a ranch house and a barn.

Sophie came out of the barn pushing a large cart as they drove up. She wheeled the cart to a pickup full of small pumpkins, then wiped one hand on her jeans and shaded her eyes with the other. When they got out of the car, Sophie smiled and waved, looking friendlier than she had at the farmers market.

"What do you think of the view?" Sophie directed their gaze beyond the barn and house to a meadow where dozens of beehives stood. The meadow followed a creek up into the forest and foothills.

"A bonny sight," Tamsin said.

"Pretty and peaceful," Scarlett agreed.

"My own piece of heaven." Sophie started moving pumpkins from the pickup to the cart. "I'm going to have to cut your visit short, though. Adam didn't show up for work today. Sorry about that." Her tone belied the apology.

Scarlett wondered if the excuse for the shorted visit accounted for Sophie's friendlier mood. But she didn't know Sophie well enough to say, and so she dismissed those thoughts as uncharitable.

"Who's Adam?" Tamsin asked.

"Adam Gray. My hired hand. He should be dealing with these pumpkins."

"For the goats?" Tamsin asked. "I grew up on a croft with sheep. They love pumpkins too. Why don't I help with the pumpkins in exchange for your time and information?"

"Thanks, but no."

Tamsin began loading pumpkins into the cart anyway. "My gran would have said no as well."

"And you ignore your gran too, don't you?" Sophie said.

"I can't ignore her anymore. She's gone. That means I can't help her anymore either, so I'm going to help you. Only today, though. I have my own work to do."

"What's your excuse?" Sophie asked Scarlett, who was helping Tamsin.

Scarlett smiled. "I don't need one."

With a few annoyed sounds from Sophie, cartful by cartful, they moved the pumpkins from the truck to storage in the barn. While they worked, Sophie told them that her land had belonged to a man named Jonathan Wright in the 1870s.

"He had orchards, bees, and goats too. I like that continuity. I used some of the materials from his house when I built mine. Wright is the one who found Robert Louis Stevenson near death along the creek. Wright or one of his sons. Stories vary."

"Do you know where they found him?" Tamsin asked.

"He was camping, so I assume in the woods farther up the creek."

When they'd emptied the truck, Sophie thanked them and asked if they'd like to see Wright's springhouse. "It's the last thing he built here that's still standing."

Tamsin eagerly agreed.

Sophie led them past the beehives toward the creek. "See the squat, brick building farther along? It's built over a cold-water spring.

It's my backup system in case my fridge dies."

"Speaking of backup systems," Scarlett said, "do you keep anything on hand in case someone reacts to a bee sting?"

"Are you expecting to have a problem?" Sophie asked.

If Sophie's hair were short enough, Scarlett thought it might bristle at the question, and that reaction almost tickled her. The ice in Sophie's blue eyes nipped Scarlett's amusement in the bud.

"Simply curious," Scarlett said. "We get lots of bees in the gardens around the museum."

"You also invite visitors. I don't," Sophie said. Her tone thawed a fraction. "We wear full beekeeping suits when we work with the hives, and I keep antihistamines on hand. Mostly I encourage people, allergic or not, to stay well away."

"I'm glad you let us come today," Tamsin said, though Scarlett saw that she took a small step back as she did. "At the market, you mentioned that someone else had asked about your land and what you know."

"And you asked if he was interested in the Stevenson story, and I said no."

"That's right," Tamsin said.

"I'm so glad we agree."

Tamsin blinked in surprise at Sophie's sarcasm, then placed a hand over her heart as her eyes filled. "You sounded exactly like my gran."

"Except for the accent," Sophie said. "Unless your gran grew up along the California coast in San Diego and Morro Bay."

"Uncanny," Tamsin said. "Gran grew up in Sandend along the coast of County of Moray."

"Close enough," Sophie said with the faintest of smiles. They'd reached the springhouse, and she patted one of its low, weathered brick walls as if it were a favorite farm animal. "It's been patched here and there, but it's not bad for 150 years old, is it?"

"That makes it a wee baby to the house I grew up in," Tamsin said. "It's 224."

Sophie stared at Tamsin without comment.

"How wonderful that we can all feel connected to history through the buildings that remain," Scarlett said, trying to ease the tension that had sprung up.

Sophie grunted, then headed back toward the farm.

"Do you know the man at the market who asked you about your land?" Scarlett asked as she and Tamsin fell in beside their hostess.

"I didn't get his name. He hasn't come out here."

"Was he in his late sixties, a bit overweight? Thinning white hair long enough to start curling above his ears?" Scarlett tried to think of anything distinctive about Quartz. "With a beard and plenty of interesting stories?"

"Stories I'm sure *he* thinks are interesting," Sophie said. "Though I suppose that would describe most men. I don't know. I was busy with paying customers, and I wasn't interested in getting to know him."

Or anyone else, including us, Scarlett thought.

"You probably need to get back to town, so I won't keep you any longer," Sophie said when they reached the drive and Scarlett's car.

"I love knowing that Stevenson spent time here," Tamsin said. "Thank you for your time."

Sophie stuffed her hands in her pockets and nodded.

"Thanks, Sophie," Scarlett said. "I hope Adam's back tomorrow."

"If he isn't, he'd better at least call in. I'd hate to lose someone who seems invested in the place, but I can't keep him on if I can't depend on him."

"You haven't heard from him?" Scarlett asked.

"I wouldn't be so angry if I had. He's also taken an interest in a young woman. She came out here a few times before I put a stop to that.

But I saw him talking to her Sunday at the market. I guess it's true that you can't get good help these days." Sophie nodded to them and walked away.

Scarlett was thankful when Tamsin said nothing more as they got in the car. She didn't need a steady flow of chatter from her passenger when her own thoughts were distracting enough. Two men weren't where they should be and hadn't let anyone know. Was it mere coincidence?

Tamsin twisted around in her seat to catch a last glimpse of the farm as they drove down the private road back to the highway. When she faced forward again, she drew in her breath sharply.

"A problem?" Scarlett asked.

"No. I thought I saw someone watching from the trees."

Scarlet turned to where Tamsin was looking. "You're kidding. Who?"

"No one," Tamsin said. "My imagination, I'm sure."

"You don't sound sure."

"I am."

Scarlett knew the words were just as much to convince Tamsin as herself.

7

Luke called the next morning as Scarlett and Cleo finished breakfast. "Good morning," he said. "Well, good enough, considering this fog didn't come in on little cat feet like Cleo's. It tromped in with clodhoppers like mine."

Scarlett took her cereal bowl to the sink and peeked out the window. "You either transported to an alternate universe or you aren't in Crescent Harbor."

"I'm still in San Francisco. I thought I'd make it here and back yesterday, but no dice. We should wrap things up this afternoon. What's new with you and Queen Cleopatra?"

"The queen is surveying her fogless realm from her perch in the living room window. She's in regal form. I am too, for that matter."

"But?"

"But Quartz is missing." Scarlett told him what little she knew about the disappearance.

"Wow. I didn't see that coming," Luke said. "Not that any of us did. Not that he did, I'm sure."

Cleo jumped from her perch in the window with a loud meow. A moment later the doorbell rang.

"Someone's at the door," Scarlett told Luke.

"Then I'll let you go."

"And let me know when you're back. Bye."

When Scarlett opened the door, she found Greta.

"I'm sorry to drop by so early," Greta said.

"No problem. Come on in. Can I get you something? Coffee? Tea? Juice?"

"I'm fine." Greta tapped the water bottle she sometimes carried at her waist during her morning walks. She sank onto the sofa, twisting her hands in her lap.

"Have you heard anything?" Scarlett asked, sitting on the other side of the sofa. She had a guess, but she knew talking things out would help Greta.

"Officers Garcia and Riggle came to the house and searched the guest room and Quartz's truck."

Scarlett frowned at the worry on Greta's face. "I guess that answers the question about whether we have to wait before reporting a missing person."

"Chief Rodriguez assured Hal it's a myth. But as far as Nina and Andy could tell, nothing in the room or the truck has been disturbed."

"How far can they tell?"

"Hal asked that. Andy said they checked for the things someone might use every day. Toothbrush, regular medications, that kind of thing. They don't know what or how much of anything Quartz brought with him, so they can't really tell if anything is missing. All they can tell is that he's tidy. His toiletries are on the dresser in the guest room, laid out as neatly as if they're on display in a historic house museum."

"You and Hal can't tell if anything is missing either?" Scarlett asked.

"No. At this point, lacking evidence to the contrary, the police are going under the assumption that Quartz disappeared against his will since he didn't take his things with him."

Scarlett felt the words like a thump to her chest, and she saw in Greta's face the effort it took to say them. "No signs of violence, though, right?"

"No, thank goodness." Greta closed her eyes. "Hal and I stewed over it all night. We hardly slept." She looked at Scarlett again. "Sometime early in the morning, Hal posed the possibility that he was taken away by water."

"Did Andy or Nina say anything to that effect?"

"No, but nothing they said negates it either. That's the kind of circular thinking we went through last night."

"Unless there was an eyewitness, there might not be any evidence to show how he was taken," Scarlett said.

"That was another strand of our thinking. It ended up as a knot we couldn't untangle. Hal finally fell asleep, and I came out for my walk."

"You said the toiletries are laid out like a display," Scarlett said. "What if it is a display of sorts? Like stage dressing? What if this disappearance is one of the clues Quartz said he'd lay out?"

"We batted around a lot of ideas, but we didn't come up with that one." Greta appeared to consider Scarlett's suggestion. "Even if that's possible, it's terribly elaborate and, frankly, a cruel joke. Why would Quartz do something like that?"

"I don't know, but we don't really know him."

"And he doesn't know us," Greta said. "Why would he orchestrate something like that to ensnare virtual strangers? What would be the point?"

"I can't think of one. Could he be a con man of some kind?"

"Of course he could. But I don't believe he is," Greta said. "On the other hand, victims of con artists don't usually believe they're being duped. But why would he do it? What could he possibly think to gain?"

"Money?"

"I don't see how," Greta said. "Nor do I want to. I like Quartz."

"I do too."

"Do you think he's a con man?" Greta asked.

"I can't picture it."

"Good." Greta stood up. "I see what you did too. You came up with a jarring thought to knock me into a better frame of mind, and it worked."

"I'm glad."

"Now I'll finish my walk and pull myself together."

"You and Hal can skip today if you'd like."

"I would not. Staying busy will pull me through this. I'll see you at the museum, Scarlett. Cleo, I'll wave to you in the window the next time I pass by."

"See you." Scarlett closed the door. She was glad Greta's mood had improved and that neither of them could picture Quartz as a con man. "But maybe he is, Cleo. What do you think? Not offering an opinion? You're wise to keep your own counsel."

Scarlett checked the time. She still had twenty minutes before she had to leave for work. She went to get one of her old field notebooks, flipping through several until she found one with plenty of blank pages. She took it and a pen back to the sofa.

"Time to get my thoughts organized, Cleo. It'll be like brainstorming. No dumb questions. No dumb suggestions. No dumb worries."

The first thing she wrote was *Adam missing?* She hadn't wanted to add to Greta's worries by mentioning an additional unexplained absence.

"Speaking of absences, Cleo, where did you leave that ball of paper I gave you yesterday?" She hadn't found bits of shredded paper around the house, so the ball might still be intact. She located it under her dresser, next to a catnip mouse.

She tossed the mouse to Cleo, who pounced on it. "Finding your treasure might be a good sign." Scarlett smoothed out the list of clues and copied them into the field notebook.

"How'd the field trip go yesterday?" Allie asked when Scarlett arrived to claim her first cup of coffee.

Scarlett felt a moment of panic. "What field trip? Did I forget a group visit?"

"I meant your trip to Left Field Farm." Allie handed a cup to Scarlett. "Either you really need this coffee, or you've had too much already. And the cool book sticking out of your purse is about to leap overboard."

Scarlett rescued the notebook and set it on the coffee shop counter. "The trip to the farm was an adventure. Quartz's disappearance is a puzzle. So is trying to figure out the clues he said he was laying out for us. I'm using one of my old field notebooks to try to organize my thoughts about all of it."

Winnie appeared as Allie pronounced the notebook not merely cool, but super cool. At Winnie's prompting, Scarlett told them about Adam's unexplained absence from the farm, Sophie's changeable moods, and Tamsin's possible watcher.

Allie tapped the notebook. "You should widen the scope of your lists. We've had a number of unusual things happen lately."

"Starting on Friday morning," Winnie said. "Finding Rylla in the closed exhibit area. The package arriving. Quartz showing up before Hal and Greta expected. We've had a multitude of surprises, and any or all of them might contribute to figuring out what's happened to Quartz."

"Just the three we want to see," Hal announced as he and Greta stepped into the shop. "They haven't found him yet, but we've had news."

"That 'yet' sounds promising," Scarlett said.

"We're trying to be optimistic," Greta said. "Officer Riggle called and told us that thanks to Scarlett's information about Quartz planning a beach walk, they've found footage from a security camera. It shows Quartz, not far from the beach, talking to a woman."

"We appreciate you letting us view the footage," Winnie said as she and Scarlett crowded around Officer Garcia's computer.

"Don't expect too much," Nina said. "It's black and white and grainy, but it still tells a story."

"A helpful story?" Scarlett asked.

"I want you to see it without being biased by my impressions."

Nina started the video and stood back as Scarlett and Winnie leaned in. She'd been right about the quality, but they recognized Quartz. He and the woman talked for several minutes. She stood with her back to the camera. The woman was impossible to identify but wore a skirt, T-shirt, and sun hat, and appeared shorter than Quartz. The talk grew animated, the woman gesturing wildly with her shoulders drawn up.

"She feels strongly about something," Scarlett said.

"Probably," Winnie said. "Think she's angry?"

"Could be," Scarlett said.

The woman yanked off her hat and threw it on the ground, then stomped away. Quartz started after her, stopped, shook his head, and went the other way. The woman passed closer to the camera, though her face still wasn't visible.

"Definitely angry," Scarlett said. "And did you see the hair? I think that's Rylla."

"She moves like Rylla," Winnie agreed.

"Can we see the stomping away again?" Scarlett asked.

Nina replayed the video.

"Rylla left the museum in a hurry yesterday with the same kind of walk," Scarlett said. "She usually has her backpack with her."

"Not at the exhibit opening," Winnie said.

"Do you know her full name?" Nina asked. "How to get hold of her?"

"Her last name is Summerville," Scarlett said. "She's an art student. I don't know where."

"She became a member at the museum, so we'll have contact information," Winnie said. "However, we have a privacy policy. I need to verify if we can share it without a warrant."

"We'll locate her through regular channels," Nina said. "If you see her at the museum again, give me a call. But don't tell her about the video."

"I wonder where she rushed off to yesterday," Scarlett said.

"Two instances of leaving a place in a hurry or a huff isn't a pattern," Winnie said. "But it's still interesting."

"She said something I didn't catch, possibly about an appointment," Scarlett said. "Greta had just told me about Quartz. I'm not sure if Rylla overheard."

Nina made a note. "There might be a connection."

"Is there a connection between Rylla, Quartz, and Adam Gray?" Scarlett told Nina about his absence. "There's no reason to believe he's really missing, though, and a connection between the three is tenuous at best."

"Tenuous is how all my favorite cases start," Nina said. "Where's the fun in easy and straightforward? But I don't mean to joke about this. The goal is to find Mr. Sutton safe and sound. So what was the Gray Ghost doing yesterday instead of working?"

"Gray Ghost?" Scarlett asked.

"Adam Gray's high school nickname," Nina said. "He was a football player with a lot of promise about ten years ago."

"Has he had any legal problems?" Winnie asked.

"None I'm aware of."

Scarlett took out her phone. "I'm calling Sophie. She might bite my head off, but perhaps she'll be willing to say if Adam showed up today." She tapped in the number. "Sophie, hi. This is Scarlett McCormick. Thank you again for having us yesterday. Can you tell me whether Adam made it there today?"

"Are you volunteering to fill in again?"

"No, I—"

"That's all right," Sophie said. "He came in. Anything else?"

Scarlett was more relieved than she'd realized she would be. Considering how irritated Sophie sounded, Scarlett didn't feel she should ask why he'd been absent. Instead, she mustered her courage to ask, "Could you describe the woman who came out to the farm to see Adam?"

"No."

The answer left Scarlett wondering whether Sophie couldn't describe the woman or if she wouldn't. She tried another question. "Have you heard about a man who's missing? Quartz Sutton?"

"No."

"Late sixties. Last seen in Crescent Harbor Monday night near the beach—"

"I'm sorry to hear it," Sophie cut in. "Why are you telling me?"

"The more people who know, the more quickly we'll find him," Scarlett said. "Do you remember anything more about the man at the market who asked about your farm?"

"He was interested in Wright's failed mine."

"You didn't tell us about a mine yesterday," Scarlett said.

"Failed mine. That sums it up."

Scarlett squelched the impulse to bristle back. "Do you remember what the man wore?"

"I'm not good with clothes, faces, or descriptions," Sophie said. "He was older. He wore a hat with fishing lures stuck in it. Ridiculous thing."

Scarlett hated to ask her last question. "What kind of failed mine?"

"Quicksilver. And I guess I'll have to do something about the mine if people are going to start coming out of the woodwork trying to find it. That's what I was talking about when I said you can get into trouble and very real danger out here. I cannot stress it enough. Abandoned mines are death traps."

8

After lunch, Scarlett took herself on a tour of the museum's galleries. She liked walking through and tried to do so several times a week. Seeing which displays visitors moved past quickly and where they spent more time helped her choose displays for the future. Rylla, for instance, spent most of her time in the *Art from the Golden Age of Illustration* exhibit. Scarlett found her there after lunch, parked in front of Wyeth's Long John Silver again.

As good a time as any to see what she knows about Quartz, Scarlett thought, *and whether or not she mentions the encounter captured in the surveillance footage. She decided not to jump immediately into those questions, though. She's into birds. I'll soften her up with a bird-watching question and go from there.*

"Rylla, hi. I bet you're just the person I should talk to. As a new bird-watcher, besides the museum gardens and my own backyard, where should I go to see them?"

"Are you kidding?" Rylla lifted her pencil from her sketchpad and stared at Scarlett. "Everywhere. The whole area. The town, Point Lobos, the marshes, the river basin—we're known for incredible bird diversity."

"Impressive. I had no idea. Do you have a favorite bird?"

"See if you can guess." Rylla took off her beanie and ran a hand from the green and iridescent blue feathers at her crown down to the violet ones around her ears.

"Ruby-throated hummingbird?"

"Too obvious, and not even close."

"So what is it?"

Rylla pulled the beanie back over her feathers. "You get one guess a day."

"And you won't tell me? But I'm a newbie at bird-watching and new to the area. Newish, anyway."

"Are you?" Rylla asked. "Cool. The library has a nice selection of bird books. Audubon is a great resource too. In exchange for that helpful advice, can I borrow Long John Silver here?"

Scarlett was taken aback by the request. "Sorry, but he has to stay put."

"Stingy."

"Me? You're as stingy as Rumpelstiltskin with the name of your favorite bird."

"Rumpelstiltskin? I love that little guy." Rylla went back to sketching.

Scarlett tried to regain Rylla's attention. "Have you seen much of Tamsin, the Scottish graduate student, since the exhibit opening? She seems pleasant. She likes the Wyeths too."

Rylla stopped sketching again. "I'll give you a reward for comparing me to my pal Rumpel, but then I need to finish my sketch. Here's one of my favorite birdsongs." She whistled a repeated sharp, sweet chirp.

"It sounds like you're saying—"

"'Cheat-cheat-cheat?' I am," Rylla said. "Ornithologists spell it with a double e, but I prefer spelling it with thoughts of dishonesty and deceit."

"I was going to say it sounds like 'sweet-sweet-sweet.'"

"Nope. If we're being honest, the sound is closer to 'cheat.' You're trying to be polite."

Scarlet forced a smile to cover her thoughts. *Is Rylla's "cheat-cheat-cheat" a veiled comment about Tamsin?*

Cleo studied Scarlett and Luke at the kitchen table, watching each mouthful they ate. Luke had returned from San Francisco in time to pick up fish tacos for supper.

"I think we're being watched," Luke said.

"Never do this." Scarlett broke off a piece of fish and gave it to Cleo. "Very bad manners. It's nice to have you back, by the way. Especially with tacos."

"I'm very glad to be back. Anything new on Quartz?"

"He appears on security footage near the beach, after he left The Salty Dog. Winnie and I got to see it."

"How's the quality?" he asked.

"Not great, but not terrible. Quartz was talking to a woman. Judging by her body language, she was angry."

"Do they have an ID?"

"Winnie and I think it might be Rylla. Nina's checking it out."

"Sounds like progress."

Scarlett's phone rang and she glanced at the display. "It's Greta. Mind if I take it?"

"Not at all. It might be more progress."

Scarlett connected. "Hi, Greta. Any news?"

"Not the good kind," Greta said. "The police are on their way here. Someone broke into Quartz's truck."

"Wow." Scarlett pictured the worry lines furrowing deeper between Greta's eyebrows. "Luke's here. Would you like us to come over? Would we be in the way?"

"Please come. Hal and I would both like the two of you here."

"We'll be there in a few minutes." When Scarlett disconnected, Luke was already wrapping their unfinished tacos.

"Want me to drive?" he asked as he put the leftovers in the refrigerator.

"I will. You just got off the road."

Scarlett's quiet Prius purred around the corner onto the street where the Barons lived. There they found officers Nina Garcia and Andy Riggle standing by Quartz's pickup. Scarlett parked in front of the house next door, and they went to ask the officers for permission to go in and keep Greta and Hal company.

"That's fine," Nina said, "but I'll tell you what I told them. The guest room is off-limits. Don't go in. Don't even peek in."

"Did someone break into the house too?" Scarlett asked.

"There's no evidence of that yet, but we'll want to check it out again."

"Understood."

"And I'm not here as an agent, but as a friend," Luke said.

"You're always welcome as a colleague or a friend," Nina said.

Hal opened the door and ushered them to the kitchen.

Greta sat at the table with her hands around a mug. "More excitement than we wanted," she said as Scarlett and Luke sat down. "And much more than Quartz probably wanted. I hope he can handle it."

Hal bowed slightly. "Can I get you something to drink?"

"What are you having, Greta?" Scarlett asked.

"Hot tea so I can warm my hands."

"That sounds lovely," Scarlett said.

"It does," Luke said.

"Warm hands all around." Hal filled three more mugs with steaming tea from a kettle and brought them to the table.

"When did it happen?" Scarlett asked.

"We don't know," Greta said. "The break-in wasn't obvious. The doors weren't hanging open and no windows were broken. Nothing like that."

"We hadn't paid much attention to the truck since the police were here yesterday," Hal said.

"Honestly, I've been avoiding it," Greta said. "That sounds silly."

"No sillier than I am. I've avoided looking in the guest room," Hal said. "As if pretending it isn't there will undo all of this. I guess it's become a kind of superstition."

"That's exactly how I feel." Greta reached over and took one of Hal's hands. "But this evening, I happened to glance in the passenger window as I walked past."

"What did you see?" Scarlett asked.

"Papers on the seat and a road map that weren't there yesterday. And the little sliding window between the cab and the topper wasn't open before, but tonight it is."

"Subtle changes," Luke said.

"Which make all the difference," Scarlett said. "Good thing you noticed them."

The doorbell rang. Hal went to answer and came back with the two police officers. Then he stood behind Greta with his hands on her shoulders.

"We've confirmed that someone went through the truck," Nina said. "Both the cab and the bed. Not someone as neat as Mr. Sutton, but certainly very careful."

"Not careful enough," Hal said.

"No, and that's good for us," Officer Riggle said. "I took photographs when we were here yesterday. We compared them to the truck's contents as they are now. The pictures prove that someone's been in the truck, but we didn't do a full inventory. Without knowing everything Mr. Sutton brought with him, we aren't able to tell if anything is missing."

"The camping gear and antique mining equipment appear to be accounted for," Nina said. "But because we can't be certain, we will state in our report that the status of the truck's contents is undetermined."

"That sounds appropriate," Greta said. "Thanks for coming so quickly."

"Of course," Andy said.

"How did they get into the truck?" Scarlett asked.

"Did you notice the rust spots on the vehicle?" Andy asked. "That speaks for the state of its security too. There's no working alarm and the lock on the camper top is a simple one."

"It would be even easier for someone to use Mr. Sutton's keys," Nina said. "Did you get your locks changed?"

"Yesterday afternoon," Hal said.

"And are you sure no one's been in the house?" Andy asked.

Hal looked toward his wife. "Greta?"

Scarlett watched Greta's face and pictured her scanning each room with her mind's eye, sifting through details.

"No. I don't think so," Greta said. "Nothing's misplaced or amiss. Neither of us has been in Quartz's room since you were here yesterday, though. If someone only went through his room, we wouldn't know."

"Do you mind if I take a look in there now?" Andy asked.

"Please do," Greta said.

Luke offered Nina his chair.

She thanked him and sat, then said, "I'm sorry about the break-in, but I'm viewing the incident as progress. Backhanded progress, I'll admit, but if the people or person responsible for Mr. Sutton's disappearance also entered the truck, then they've given us more to work with.

The more they give us, the more likely we are to catch them."

"You have a sunny perspective on this situation, Nina." Hal squeezed Greta's shoulders and resumed his seat. "We're trying for that too, but sometimes we slip."

"It helps me love my job," Nina said. "Now, what can you tell me about the package that arrived for Mr. Sutton? I can't help but wonder if it has something to do with all of this."

"That wouldn't surprise me," Scarlett said, and the others echoed the sentiment. "As far as I know, he wasn't willing to share any specific information about it, though."

"Interesting." Nina took out her notebook. "You don't know what was in it?"

"No," Hal said. "And that means we don't know whether the contents are here or gone."

"And if they're gone," Greta said, "we don't know if Quartz has them with him or if the burglar took them. Is it burglary if someone uses keys to get into a truck?"

"If the keys aren't come by legally, yes," Nina said. "So if this burglary is connected to the package, then it's safe to say the burglar knows Mr. Sutton and knows or suspects what's in the package. Did he give you any information about it at all?"

"He called it his treasure," Scarlett said. "He might have been laughing at himself, though."

"He seemed happy to—wait," Hal corrected himself. "Seems happy to laugh at himself."

"He calls himself secretive," Greta said. "He said he'd been laying out clues and would keep giving them to us."

"So he wants you to figure out what it is?" Nina asked.

"If we don't, he said 'in the end, all will be revealed,'" Scarlett said. "Is any of that helpful?"

"Everything is, even if it's not immediately clear how. Have you had any luck deciphering the clues?"

"I'm not even sure what is a clue and what isn't," Greta said.

Scarlett, Hal, and Luke shook their heads.

Andy appeared in the kitchen doorway. "I can't see that anything has been disturbed. I compared the room to the pictures from yesterday. Nothing appears to be shifted or rearranged."

"Thank goodness," Greta said. "The thought of someone pawing through things in here is almost nauseating."

"Besides the four of you, do you know who else interacted with Mr. Sutton since he's been in town?" Andy asked.

"Allie Preston at Burial Grounds," Scarlett said.

"Quartz came to the exhibit opening at the museum Friday night," Hal said. "He spent most of his time with the paintings, but chatted with a few people. No one for long."

"He might have talked to Sophie Morata at the farmers market," Scarlett said.

"No-nonsense woman?" Nina asked. "Has a farm east of town?"

"That's Sophie," Scarlett said. "She said a man at the market asked her about an old quicksilver mine on her land. I wondered if it was Quartz. Luke and I saw him at the market, but Sophie could only say he was an older man with a fishing hat. I don't remember seeing Quartz with one."

Greta and Hal agreed.

"He mentioned a hat Friday night," Luke said. "He said it had the air of a desperado."

"So that probably wasn't him asking about Sophie's mine," Andy said.

"Sophie's definitely no-nonsense about people poking around her land," Scarlett said. "I took Tamsin out there yesterday at Sophie's invitation, but I still thought she might run us off."

"Tamsin's the Scottish graduate student who came to the opening, isn't she?" Hal asked. "Quartz chatted with her, then seemed to avoid her."

"Really?" Nina asked.

"I can't be sure," Hal said, "but I spent most of my time watching him the same way I watch good actors."

"Do you think he was playing a part?" Andy asked.

"That didn't occur to me. I often watch people that way for mannerisms and such I can copy to lend authenticity to my roles."

"He's also fairly nosy." Greta smiled at her husband.

"Anything else to add before we take off?" Nina asked.

"It might be nothing," Scarlett said, "but when Hal mentioned Quartz and Tamsin at the exhibit opening, it reminded me of Rylla. She was there, and I think she ended up avoiding Tamsin too."

⁂

As Scarlett unlocked her front door, her stomach growled.

"I guess we should reheat the tacos," Luke said.

"Of course we should, if for no other reason than for Cleo's entertainment."

They zapped the leftovers in the microwave and sat down.

Cleo took up her position, flicking her tail as she waited for them to start eating.

"Is she going to watch us the whole time?" Luke asked.

"It's a hobby of hers where seafood is concerned."

"It's more than a hobby," Luke said. "I think she's an authority on watching—"

"Whoa. Watching." Scarlett set down her taco. "I almost forgot. Tamsin thought someone was watching us from the trees at Left Field Farm yesterday."

"Creepy."

Scarlett gave Cleo a piece of fish. "I'd like to see that security footage of Quartz again."

"Why?"

"It just occurred to me that I saw him do something that might be important. If we can see the footage tonight, will you come with me? I'd like to see if you catch it too."

"Sure. I wanted to view that footage anyway."

Scarlett called Andy, who agreed to play the video for them. After she and Luke finished eating, spoiling Cleo with a few more bites, they drove to the station. Andy set up the footage and stayed to watch too.

"There," Scarlett said. "Right before Quartz walks away. See that? What's he doing?"

"Lifting his right hand," Andy said.

"In a wave," Luke said. "As though greeting someone."

"Yes," Scarlett said. "So who was watching them?"

9

"Shark attack," Allie said, handing Scarlett her first cup of coffee the following morning. She leaned across the counter and pointed at the dark semicircles under her eyes. "See these bags? Want to know why they're there? Because with all his talk about cute and fascinating sea critters, Quartz threw in questions about jellyfish stings, sea otter bites, and shark attacks. So all last night, stinging, biting critters swam through my dreams nipping at me."

"Yikes."

"It's okay." Allie took a sip of her own coffee. "I'll get over it. But it made me think. What if Quartz was gathering information, or courage, before swimming out to a boat?"

"Staging his own disappearing act? Great minds, Allie. I wondered about staging, and Greta and I Ial pondered about someone nabbing him by boat. Combine the two and we have your idea."

"But could either of those happen off our beach without witnesses? Even at night there's usually someone there."

"It seems far-fetched," Scarlett said, "but so is his disappearance. Oh, and now someone's broken into his truck. What could a down-on-his-luck retired teacher have that's worth kidnapping him for?"

"Down on his luck?"

"That's why Greta's friend Henry asked if Quartz could stay with them."

"Whether he has money doesn't matter," Allie said. "Not if he has wealthy relatives or friends. Has there been a ransom demand?"

"We haven't heard about one, and we might not, depending on who receives it. But what if his luck changed—or someone thinks it did? What if he found something valuable in an abandoned mine?"

"The police will think of every possible scenario," Allie said. "Right?"

"Right, but Nina says everything helps, so—"

"So I should call Nina and tell her about Quartz's critter questions? I'll share our thoughts on improved luck, ransoms, and abandoned mines too."

"It can't hurt," Scarlett said.

"Here come Greta and Hal." Allie nodded toward the museum's front door. "Hi, you two. Coffee?"

"Two cups of your finest," Hal said. "What do you think, Scarlett? Do we look more chipper this morning?"

Scarlett's heart skipped a beat. "Have you had news?"

"Hal, dear," Greta chided, putting her arm through his. "I told you that question needed a preface."

Hal sighed theatrically as he took the cup Allie handed him. "I should always listen to you. Why do I ever forget? I'm sorry to say there's nothing new on the Quartz front. The change is with us. Last night, after everyone left, we decided that Nina's view of progress is the cork we need to plug the hole from whence our optimism had begun to leak and trickle down the drain."

"I see," Allie said. "Sounds, uh, fun?"

"This is his fourth cup of coffee this morning," Greta said.

Hal nodded several times. "Nina's view of progress is solid, though."

"Because everything helps?" Allie asked. "Scarlett just passed that tip along. It should be our motto."

"I second that," Hal said.

"So here's a point of progress," Scarlett said. "Something occurred to me on the way home last night." She told them about viewing the security footage again. "Andy and Luke agreed that Quartz might have waved to someone right at the end of the video."

"But can they find that person?" Allie asked.

"Maybe not," Greta said. "But now we know there's someone else out there who might know something."

Hal raised his coffee cup. "To progress."

Greta's phone rang, and Hal jumped, almost sloshing his coffee.

"Oh dear," Greta said. "It's Henry. I never called him."

"We're here for you, and the museum isn't open yet," Hal said. "Put it on speaker."

Greta set the call to speaker. "Henry—"

"Greta, the Crescent Harbor Police called me. I thought Quartz was already back home. I certainly didn't expect to hear he's a missing person. Why didn't you call me?"

"I'm so sorry you found out that way, Henry," Greta said. "We gave your name to the police. They're talking to anyone who might be able to shed light on what's happened. My only excuse for not calling is that I assumed the police would want to talk to you first."

The man sighed. "Yes, that makes sense. I apologize, Greta. I shouldn't have complained. I must be in shock."

"Amen to that. None of us knows what to do."

"And regrettably, as fond as I am of Quartz, I wasn't much help to the police. I'm not in frequent contact with him. I felt completely useless after I hung up."

"We all do," Greta said. "To throw more bad news at you, someone broke into his truck."

"Is that connected to his disappearance?" Henry asked.

"We don't know."

"Is Crescent Harbor usually rife with crime?"

"Not at all," Greta insisted.

"Henry, this is Hal," her husband chimed in. "We have you on speakerphone. Do you know who Quartz came to see here?"

"I wish I did, Hal."

"He's here on behalf of a museum, isn't he?" Greta asked. "Would they know?"

"It's a small museum," Henry said. "Your 'they' is pretty much Quartz."

Hal asked, "Do you know if he knows anyone else around this area?"

"Sorry. The police asked me these questions too. I'll check with our mutual friends up here, but otherwise I have no answers. Please keep me posted on what's going on."

Scarlett moved closer to the phone. "Henry? This is Scarlett McCormick, a friend of Greta and Hal. And Quartz. Do you think Quartz would explore an abandoned mine on his own?"

After a hesitation, Henry asked, "Have you heard him call himself an old fool?"

"Yes."

"Well, old fools always think they know better than silly things like safety regulations."

<hr />

At lunchtime, on the way to eat her sandwich in the museum gardens, Scarlett found herself back at the coffee shop. "I spend an awful lot of time in your java den, Allie. Perhaps I should just move my desk in here."

"Why don't I arrange a pipeline directly to your office?" Allie said.

"Fabulous."

Allie waved at someone behind Scarlett. "Hello, Tamsin. Goodness, what's wrong?"

"My flat." Tamsin had the red eyes and swollen nose of someone who'd recently cried, and she sounded near tears again.

"Flat tire?" Allie asked.

"No, my apartment. Someone broke in. My laptop's been stolen. And I don't know if I should be afraid or not, but if I tell my parents they'll say I should come home."

"I'm so sorry," Scarlett said. "Have you called the police?"

"They were very kind, but it's highly unlikely that they'll recover it."

"Did they say that?" Allie asked.

"No, but I've read the statistics. Mum insisted on it before I came. She and Dad have frightful imaginations fueled by watching too many American crime shows."

"When did it happen?" Scarlett asked.

Allie handed Tamsin a coffee. "On the house."

"Thank you." Tamsin blew her nose. "I went for a run. The police say it might have been someone who knows my routine. Or someone who saw me leave."

"What about your research?" Scarlett asked. "Is it all on the laptop?"

Tamsin took a sip of coffee then a deep breath. "Yes, but it's backed up in cloud storage, thank goodness." She dug in a pocket and held out a flash drive. "And on this. Everything but some emails are backed up in both places—and those emails sounded weird. They hinted at someone having a lost Stevenson manuscript."

"Anything else missing from the apartment?" Allie asked.

Tamsin shook her head.

"What made the emails weird?" Scarlett asked.

"They were anonymous, and the sender wanted to sell the manuscript directly to me. I assume they found me through my correspondence with the Robert Louis Stevenson Society. I also assume it's a scam, but I kept the emails thinking I might use them for an article down the road."

"They aren't such a great loss, then," Allie said.

"No. But here's why I really am afraid." Tamsin's voice quavered. "Before I came here, I stopped at the library and used a computer to check my cloud account."

"And?" Allie asked.

"And I've been stupid. I set the account to remember me and open without a username or password if it's accessed from my laptop. My research is intact. That's the important thing. I know it is. But I'd backed up those emails in the cloud, and that file is gone. Deleted."

"What about the original emails in your inbox?"

"Those are gone too."

"That is scary," Scarlett said. "If you haven't already, I'd recommend telling the police about this."

Tamsin took a shuddering breath. "You're right. I will. Thank you again for the coffee." She left the shop.

Watching her go, Scarlett said, "I wonder if she's going to tell them right now."

"I hope she does," Allie said. "Because somehow I can't quite buy the coincidence of two burglaries."

Tamsin's news changed Scarlett's mood. Rather than eat lunch in the gardens, she went back to her office where she could think while listening to soft jazz. The mathematical progressions she heard in musical arrangements sometimes helped arrange her thoughts. Exercise could help with that too, and she decided to climb the winding stairs to the cupola at the top of the museum's clock tower after lunch. The climb would be more strenuous than a stroll through the gardens, especially done several times in a row.

More anxiety-burning too, Scarlett reflected on her way to the tower.

With each clanging step up the spiraling iron staircase, Scarlett worked through her questions about Tamsin. For someone who backed up her research in several places, as one should, why hadn't she done that with the emails? Who'd stolen her laptop, found her cloud account, and deleted the emails? Could Tamsin have deleted them herself?

Another disquieting question entered her mind: *Had the emails existed at all?*

It wasn't in Scarlett's nature to distrust people. *Mistrust and distrust feed into unhappiness*, she thought. *It's worse if you add them to disquiet, apprehension, and uneasiness.*

She climbed to the top of the tower, above the tops of the palms in the gardens, then went back down and up again to work out her worries. When she was once more at the top, breathing hard and feeling each heartbeat, she gazed out at the ocean. The vastness of the water, with so many shifting shades of blue, put her worries in perspective. She and her questions were so small, and she found that insignificance calming. Scarlett took in the magnificent view for a few more minutes, then descended and went to find Winnie.

"Got a minute for an update on Quartz?" Scarlett had found Winnie in the security office in the basement.

"Sure thing." Winnie sat before a bank of monitors displaying video feeds from around the museum. She swiveled to face Scarlett and waved at the chair beside her. "Have a seat. What's new?"

Scarlett sat and brought her up to speed on the two burglaries and Quartz's wave at the end of the surveillance footage. She didn't mention her questions about Tamsin. Without proof, she didn't trust her distrust.

"We have a jumbled jigsaw puzzle in front of us," Winnie said. "Lots of pieces and no clear idea where they go. Good catch on the wave. It might be the clue that *waves* the day."

Scarlett groaned. "That's awful."

"You're just jealous that you didn't think of it." Winnie swiveled back to the monitors and pointed at one. "That camera is in the gallery with the illustration exhibit. Recognize anyone?"

Scarlett studied the small gathering. "Rylla. She's certainly industrious."

"She likes hats too. She's wearing a different one today."

"Interesting," Scarlett said. "I think my grandfather had a hat like that. It was his favorite fishing hat."

Winnie put her fingertips to her forehead. "I see you musing on the coincidence of two burglaries and two fishing hats."

"You're a mind reader."

"Keep in mind that there are boatloads of burglaries in the world," Winnie said. "And even more fishing hats."

"I will, but I also think I'll go say hi to Rylla." *And what else?* Scarlett mused on her way to the gallery. *Nothing about the security footage of her with Quartz. No point in spooking her.*

Rylla, engrossed in sketching, simply lifted a shoulder in response to Scarlett's greeting.

Scarlett took advantage of that concentration to examine Rylla's hat. There were no fishing lures stuck in it, but without leaning closer and staring, she couldn't tell if there were holes where lures had been. "You know an old guy named Quartz, don't you, Rylla?"

"Not all that old, but sure."

"You know he's missing?" Scarlett caught a quick glance from Rylla. She couldn't tell if Rylla had guessed the question carried more meaning than Scarlett's light tone gave away. "I'm worried about him. I like him."

"He's nice enough."

"I visited Left Field Farm this week. Quartz would like it. It's a beautiful place. If I could, I'd paint that landscape."

"You should try," Rylla said.

"My mother could paint it. I'm better at manual labor. Tamsin came with me to the farm, and we ended up pitching in with the chores because the hired hand wasn't there."

Rylla said nothing. She was busy erasing lines and redrawing them.

"Do you know Adam Gray?"

"Sorry, no." Rylla started packing her materials away.

"Did you hear that someone broke into Tamsin's apartment?" Scarlett asked, thinking one of the compartments of Rylla's backpack was the right size for a laptop.

"What is this, the case of the curious curator?" Rylla slung the backpack over her shoulder.

"Wait. Don't I get another guess at your favorite bird?"

"Not today." On her way to the door, Rylla raised her voice. "I don't have to answer any of your questions."

10

Scarlett sat at her desk, berating herself for the inept way she'd questioned Rylla. *Clumsy, clumsy, clumsy.* The repetition reminded her of Rylla's whistled birdsong, *cheat-cheat-cheat.* Maybe Rylla's song hadn't been a veiled comment on Tamsin. Maybe it had been self-reflection. *How honest is Rylla?*

Wanting to regain the serenity she'd felt in the clock tower's cupola, Scarlett switched on the soft jazz again. She closed her eyes and sat back in her chair with its buttery, soft leather. *Everyone makes mistakes. I'm not an expert in interrogation. I'm a museum professional who should attend to her own job.* She was also a museum professional who heard whispers at her door.

"Is she asleep?" Hal's voice asked quietly.

"Shh," Greta answered. "If she is, then she obviously needs the nap."

"Not napping," Scarlett said with a laugh. "Call it a meditation. Come on in."

"Allie told us about Tamsin's break-in and the missing emails." Greta watched Hal collapse in one of the visitor chairs. "And he's coming down off his caffeine buzz."

Scarlett rubbed her temples. "I'm so frustrated that I don't recognize the clues Quartz laid out for us. Do we know him well enough to understand how his mind works? Do we need to understand him to get his clues? Do we know if he'd finished laying them out?"

"We've been over that," Greta said. "We decided he wouldn't have had time to lay them all out."

"We did," said Hal. "And we decided we'll do the best we can with what we have. Positivity and progress go hand in hand."

"I think Quartz would approve of that," Greta said. "And so do I. What do you have in the way of clues so far, Scarlett?"

"Nothing very coherent, but I'm happy to share." Scarlett took her field notebook from her purse.

"That's beautiful," Hal said.

"Isn't it? It makes me feel vaguely historic. Wait." Scarlett brought out her phone, took pictures of the pages with her notes, then tapped and swiped. "There. Old school meets new school. Now you have my notes. I sent them to Allie, Winnie, and Luke too."

Hal and Greta pulled out their phones and started reading.

"You've noted that Quartz spent more time with the Parrish and Wyeth illustrations at the opening," Hal said. "Especially Long John Silver."

"According to Luke."

"An astute observation," Hal said. "But is it a clue?"

"Tamsin's in Crescent Harbor to research Stevenson," Greta said. "Is that a clue or a coincidence?"

"And how do her anonymous emails about a lost Stevenson manuscript fit in?" Hal asked. "Emails which are now lost themselves."

"I hate to say it, but were they real or a scam?" Scarlett asked.

"What kind of scam?" Greta asked.

"And scamming who?" Scarlett got up and paced. "I have no idea. That's why I hate to say it. In fact, I didn't say anything to Winnie about it."

"Something prompted your thoughts, though," Greta said.

"And your pacing," said Hal.

"So let's explore this." Greta regarded Scarlett the way she must have regarded a student who needed to revise and develop the premise of her essay.

"Maybe Tamsin erased the emails or she made up the story about them altogether," Scarlett said. "But I'm being suspicious based on no evidence whatsoever." She reached the office door and whirled around. "Except we think both Rylla and Quartz avoided Tamsin. I'm sure she needled Rylla deliberately. Why or to what end, I don't know. But none of that is enough to label her suspicious or a scammer." She dropped into a chair.

"No, no." Hal waved his hand at Scarlett. "Keep pacing. It was helping you think. I know it helps me. Like working through blocking for a theater production."

Scarlett stayed put. "Sorry, Hal. That's all I've got on Tamsin." She straightened in the chair. "Actually, thinking about Tamsin is what prompted me to check the surveillance footage again." She told them about Tamsin's report of a watcher in the woods. "She thought she saw someone. Then said she was sure she hadn't, but her turnabout wasn't convincing. How's that for a mush of did, didn't, maybe, and might?"

"Maybe mush is what she's after," Hal said. "If she's conning us."

"To what end?" Greta asked. "I haven't gotten that feeling from her at all."

"We haven't spent as much time with her as Scarlett."

"I've spent some time with her," Scarlett said. "But I don't know her well enough to be making any accusations."

"They're hardly accusations," Greta said. "We form opinions about the people we meet. That's a natural part of human behavior. I'm simply playing devil's advocate."

"We're working our way through a puzzle," Hal said. "We've done this kind of thing before. We have to examine the pieces from all angles."

"Winnie called it a jumbled jigsaw puzzle," Scarlett said.

"Make a note of your observations and concerns about Tamsin," Greta said. "Remember, everything helps."

Hal scrolled through Scarlett's notebook pages on his phone. "Didn't you love trying to guess what was in Christmas presents when you were a kid? Squeezing them. Shaking. Weighing." He mimed hefting something in his hand. "I was awfully good at it."

"Hal?" Greta asked. "Where is this non sequitur leading you?"

"The mystery package. Its size and shape. We can't squeeze or shake it, and we don't know the weight because we didn't hold it."

"We saw Winnie holding it," Scarlett said. "She held it carefully, but it didn't appear terribly heavy." A knock at her office door drew her attention. "Nice timing, Winnie. Come in."

Winnie entered. "I got the pictures of your notebook pages. So, what did you see me holding? Remember, I'm not terribly large, but I am mighty."

"Quartz's package," Hal said.

"Ah. That took no might at all," Winnie said. "It was less than a pound. Probably not more than half a pound. I didn't shake the package, of course, but nothing moved around inside. There was no rattling or shifting of contents when I picked it up."

"She's good," Hal said.

"Whether it held one item or several, it was packaged carefully," Winnie said.

"So it might have been small pieces or parts belonging to a larger piece of mining equipment," Hal said. "Replacement parts?"

"Why would Quartz have any parts sent here?" Winnie asked.

"Excellent question," Hal said. "Maybe he was hoping to find something in addition to old mining equipment. Because, really, how much old mining equipment is there to be found in or around Crescent Harbor?"

"Danielle at The Vintage Idiot might know," Scarlett suggested. "Or know how to find out."

"She might have an idea who Quartz came to get the stuff from too," Winnie said. "Good suggestion. Why don't you give her a call?"

"I find it better talking to Danielle in person," Hal said.

"Better?" Winnie asked.

"Any excuse to visit her shop," Greta said.

Scarlett grabbed her purse. "Let's go."

The Vintage Idiot held more merchandise than seemed possible from the outside of the building. Danielle Jensen, owner and operator, knew where to find every bit of her stock. She also knew how to make the stuffed shelves, cabinets, corners, and tables attractive and accessible. She specialized in vintage everything—chrome dinette sets, eight-track tapes and players, and lunch boxes from the 1960s, '70s, and '80s. She also had collectible plates and figurines, pop culture novelties of all kinds, and funky jewelry she often sold straight from around her own neck and wrists.

When Scarlett, Greta, and Hal walked through The Vintage Idiot's door that afternoon, Danielle was groaning with pleasure as she slid her feet into a pair of slippers sporting plush, whiskered tiger heads. "I always pay when I start the day in heels," she said. "These will soothe my savage beasts and still work well with the outfit, don't you think?" The outfit in question was leopard-print leggings, a zebra-striped tunic, and a necklace of chunky amber beads.

"I wish I could carry off that style half as well," Hal said.

"You let me know when you're ready to try, Hal, and I'll fix you up. Now, what can I do for you three?"

Hal took the lead. "What do you know about old mining equipment that might be found around here, if there is any?"

"Next to nothing about it, but I know who you need to talk to." Danielle went behind her sales counter and began to flip through a vintage rolodex next to the cash register. "As for whether there is any to be found, ask yourself how many antique spyglasses you would expect to find."

"Not many," Scarlett said.

"And yet," Danielle said, "I have tons."

"How have I missed seeing spyglasses on your shelves?" Hal asked. "Greta, are you thinking what I'm thinking?"

"That a spyglass would make a great birthday present for Miguel?" Miguel was the Barons' seven-year-old grandson.

"Well, I was thinking for me, but yes, I'm sure Miguel would love one too."

"One for each of you makes sense to me," Danielle said. "Here's who you need to call about mining equipment. Virgil Soto. He's local. Want the phone number?"

"And two spyglasses to go, please," Greta said.

Scarlett stepped outside to call Virgil Soto while Greta and Hal chose their spyglasses. When they came out of the shop with their purchases, Scarlett asked if they minded making a detour on the way back to the museum.

"Whither are we wandering?" Hal asked.

"Virgil Soto's," Scarlett said as the three climbed back into the Barons' SUV. "He invited us to stop by."

Scarlett read off the address Virgil had given her, praying the lead wouldn't prove to be a dead end. Virgil had sounded delighted at the prospect of visitors. But Scarlett had to wonder if they'd learn anything that would lead to Quartz.

Virgil's address took them inland a mile or two, to a street lined with modest older bungalows. Hal parked in front a weathered one that gave the impression of being in a black-and-white photograph.

As they mounted the front steps, Scarlett could see the front porch was in need of a good sweep.

A man in his late seventies or early eighties with a fringe of light-gray hair answered Scarlett's knock. His wide smile and great brush of a mustache brought warmth and color back to the picture. "You must be Scarlett and company," he said with his thumbs hooked in the suspenders holding up his worn work pants. "I'm Virgil. Come on in. We'll sit in the parlor."

They followed him into a spotless room with a potbellied stove. The walls were covered in narrow shelves, each shelf filled with mechanical contraptions. Scarlett couldn't tell what most of them were or did. The brass, glass, and gears of each one gleamed with attentive dusting or polishing.

"You have your own museum," Scarlett said. Catching sight of a spyglass, she nudged Hal, who wandered over to look more closely.

"Some of the gadgets here are old enough for a museum," Virgil said. "I'm one of them." He cackled and sat in a rocker with the plain wooden slats that marked it as Mission style and possibly another museum piece. "The rest of these gizmos I made myself."

"They're beautiful," Greta said, turning in a circle as she gazed at them. "What do they do?"

"Keep my hands and head busy, mostly. Strain my eyes. Some are banks. Some tell time. Most just whir, whiz, whirl, and ring. You'll find another chair in the kitchen, young fella."

Scarlett and Greta sat in the two chairs near the stove, exchanging a grin over Hal being referred to as "young fella." Hal came back with the other.

"I got interested in old mines and did a bit of collecting," Virgil continued. "You don't collect much of that kind of equipment before you run out of room, though. So I switched gears, as it were." He chuckled.

"Your friend Quartz helped me out by clearing the last of my mining collection off my kitchen table. I sure did hate to hear he's missing."

"How did you hear about it?" Scarlett asked.

"The police came around. I told them what I know. Wasn't much."

"Did Quartz mention knowing anyone else in the area?" Greta asked.

"We talked and enjoyed ourselves. Didn't get around to trading names of acquaintances. The police showed me pictures they took from inside his truck. The pieces I gave him are all there."

"We tracked you down through Danielle Jensen at The Vintage Idiot," Hal said. "I guess we should have asked the police."

"The police are always a good place to start," Virgil said. "They're careful, though. Don't give away the secrets up their sleeves."

"You're not a secret, are you?" Greta asked.

"No ma'am. I'm a retired lineman for the power company. That's how I got interested in old mines. We had to keep an eye out for unmarked mines. Dangerous places."

"We keep hearing that," Scarlett said.

"Believe it."

Scarlett did. She couldn't imagine the kind of trouble one might find in a place like that. "Do you know anyone in the area who explores old mines?"

"Only fools."

"Quartz sometimes called himself an old fool," Greta said.

"Getting the jab in first." Virgil rapped his knuckles on the rocker's arm. "The young dismiss old folks. They assume we've lived past our sell-by dates. Hear me on this. Quartz is no fool."

"Thank you," Greta said. "You've affirmed what we believe too."

"Did you see Quartz near the beach Monday evening, by any chance?" Scarlett asked.

"I don't often get out to my own porch, much less the beach.

Too hard on the knees and hips."

"What did you and Quartz talk about?" Hal asked.

"Pirate stories." He laughed at the surprised silence that followed his words. "You didn't expect that, did you? I don't remember how we got onto pirates. It was one of those long looping conversations that's hard to track back."

"That sounds exactly like Quartz," Greta said.

"Thank you for all your help, Virgil," Scarlett said, rising.

On their way to the door, Virgil said, "I'd love to get over to the museum one day soon. I'd like to see that exhibit Quartz likes so much—hold on. Our jabber didn't loop. We went straight from the exhibit to pirates. Sorry about that. My memory isn't usually so full of holes. Worrying over Quartz has made it worse. And now you'll think I'm an old fool, but I know there's something I wanted to tell Quartz the next time I see him. For the life of me, I can't think of what it was. But I have a feeling it was important."

11

Scarlett put the finishing touches on supper while talking to Luke on speakerphone. "We're having cheesy scalloped potatoes from the recipe my mother perfected decades ago."

"That sounds amazing."

"And a crisp green salad full of tomatoes, avocado, and mushrooms." She stopped slicing vegetables and focused on the sounds coming from the phone. "I hear seagulls in the background. Where are you? I thought you were coming over for dinner."

"I am. I'm walking," Luke said. "It's a beautiful evening. What's the latest on Quartz?"

"Nothing really."

"Spinning your wheels?"

Scarlett pictured Virgil's bright brass and glass contraptions. "More like whirling. That's not the same as spinning."

"Definitely not. Whirling suggests you have things going on upstairs."

"Lots of things." Scarlett wiped her hands on a dish towel, then whirled it. Luke couldn't see the towel, but Cleo showed her approval by trying to catch it. "Things are also whizzing and there's a good bit of whirring. Unless the whirring is really Cleo purring. Is that you ringing the doorbell?"

"It is, and after the walk and hearing about all that activity, I'm starving."

Scarlett and Cleo answered the door. Luke scooped up the cat before she made a break for the lovely evening.

"Cleo will supervise while you set up the TV trays," Scarlett said. "Then come get your plate."

"Does Cleo get a tray too?"

"No," Scarlett said from the kitchen. "And please don't give her ideas. Do you mind putting your FBI hat back on for a minute?"

"Hat on."

"We hear and read about women of all ages going missing. But old men? Who grabs them?"

Luke leaned against the kitchen doorframe. "It might not be that nefarious."

"Then what?" Scarlett asked.

"Medical emergency?"

"The police checked area hospitals."

"He'd only be in a hospital if someone found him," Luke said. "But if his beach walk took him farther afield than we imagine, maybe he hasn't been found."

"There are plenty of places in the hills and along the coast where people could get into trouble," Scarlett said. "But could Quartz really walk so far out that someone hasn't come across him yet? And if he's been lying there all this time . . ." Her voice got higher as that picture formed in her head.

"Hey, hey." Luke put his arms around her. "It's a possibility, but it seems unlikely. The police will have that kind of search well in hand."

"I know. And I'm all right." She leaned into him then pulled away and filled two plates. "I'm still going to wrap up in the afghan while we watch the movie, though."

"What movie did you get?"

"*The Lady Vanishes*. Not because I want to pick up tips for locating people who've vanished, but because it has a happy ending. And I really, really hope there's a happy ending to Quartz's story."

That night, Scarlett dreamed that Quartz walked away from her, then turned and waved at someone behind her. She spun around to see someone wearing a fishing hat chock-full of feathers disappearing around a corner. Scarlett ran to catch up with Quartz. Stumbling, she slipped off the path and found herself sinking in quicksand. First to her ankles, then to her knees, then to her hips. She yelled for Quartz. But all she saw was his hand waving feebly as the quicksand sucked him down too.

Scarlett woke to crows cawing somewhere in the neighborhood. She reached for Cleo but found an empty hollow on the covers where the cat had been curled beside her. Scarlett checked her phone. It was almost time for the alarm anyway. She got up and stood under a warm shower, washing away the last sickly sensations of quicksand from her skin and hair.

While she ate breakfast, a text arrived from Greta. *Can we meet for coffee at the museum a little earlier than usual?*

Sure, Scarlett sent back. *Have you heard something?*

No. I have an idea.

We need all of those we can get.

Scarlett felt better knowing that Allie, Greta, and Hal hadn't slept any better than she had. Eyes drooped and hands covered yawns.

"No fair," Allie said. "Where's Winnie? Is she getting more sleep than we are?"

"She's in the middle of a five-mile run," Greta said.

"Show-off," Allie griped. "May I have dibs on going first? I'll only take a few minutes, then I'll get the coffee going for you guys and the rest of my adoring public."

"Go for it," Greta said.

"I've been rethinking the idea of Quartz swimming out to a boat," Allie said. "Unless he had a wet suit, he'd risk hypothermia. He didn't rent one. I checked around."

"Good thinking," Scarlett said.

"Succumbing to hypothermia is a possibility, then," Greta said.

"Sure, but it's a remote one," Allie said. "He doesn't have the physique of a tremendous swimmer, and unless he's a tremendous actor, he doesn't seem like the kind of guy to stage his own disappearance."

"What do you think, Hal?" Scarlett asked. "Is Quartz a tremendous actor?"

"Storytellers often are," Hal said. "And there's no doubt he's a terrific storyteller. He has the voice and the timing to capture his audience. Even his eyes draw people in." He rubbed his chin. "But no, Quartz is a front-porch, rocking-chair kind of storyteller. His listeners sit at his feet. Or across the dinner table. He doesn't need the depth and breadth of a stage to spin his tales. He's a collector and a raconteur. I really don't see him fabricating and arranging his own disappearance."

Greta's phone vibrated in her messenger bag. She pulled it out and checked the display. "Henry." She answered, and it became clear that he wanted an update. From the number of times Greta paused for his interruptions, the others gathered he was as worried and impatient as they were.

"Put him on speaker again," Allie suggested.

"Henry? Henry. Hold on a moment. I'm putting you on speakerphone. Four heads are better than my sleep-deprived one." She tapped the button.

"Four?" Henry repeated. "Did Hal suddenly sprout two extra heads?"

"We're at the Reed Museum with the curator and the purveyor of perfect coffee," Hal said. "We're a team. Tell us what's on your mind."

"I called your police station and got the brush-off. I'm concerned that they aren't taking this matter seriously."

"The Crescent Harbor police aren't like that, Henry," Greta said. "They're doing everything they can."

"But is it leading to anything useful?" Henry demanded. "I can't concentrate on my lecture notes. I'm sleepwalking through meetings. How hard is it to find one old man?"

"Henry," Hal said, "listen to me. Wise words coming your way. Are you ready?"

"Yes."

"'How poor are they that have not patience!' *Othello*. You see, Henry? Shakespeare knows all."

Henry gave a bark of laughter. "You're right, Hal. Thank you. I'll do my best to be patient. Keep me posted."

"He's a fellow thespian," Hal explained to Scarlett and Allie as Greta disconnected.

"Now for my idea," Greta said. "There's one small tour today, and Hal offered to handle it while I research the truth behind lost Stevenson manuscripts on my trusty laptop." Greta patted the messenger bag.

"Quartz mentioned lost manuscripts Saturday night at supper," Hal said. "Tamsin claims she received emails offering to sell her one."

"Quartz said that half of Stevenson's manuscripts are missing." Greta shook her head. "Half. What happened to them?"

"What a tragedy if it's true," Allie said.

Greta lowered her voice, although the museum wasn't open. "I also wonder if Tamsin could be several steps ahead of us in the same research. What if she's only posing as a graduate student while she's actually searching for a lost manuscript?"

"And Quartz somehow got in the way?" Scarlett knew she sounded skeptical.

"I warned Greta about jumping to conclusions," Hal said. "She wisely reminded me of our motto. Everything helps."

"Absolutely right," Scarlett said. "I didn't mean to cast doubt. Do you want to work in my office?"

"The cataloging workroom in the basement is fine. It'll be quiet and I'll be out of your hair. I'll find you if I come up with anything."

Scarlett shared Luke's thoughts on the possibility of Quartz lying injured and undiscovered within walking distance of downtown Crescent Harbor. She kept her quicksand nightmare to herself.

When the meeting adjourned, she yawned and took a cup of coffee upstairs to her office.

"And you will sit down and take joy in doing your actual museum work," she told herself. Since she loved her job, it wasn't hard to follow through on that directive. She spent the next few hours researching a future special exhibit that would highlight the art and music of mid-fourteenth-century Europe—the plague years. Despite reading gruesome details of the Black Death, she found the routine of research soothing. When Greta and Winnie knocked at her door shortly before lunch, she felt quite refreshed.

"I found more than one reference to the idea that half of Stevenson's manuscripts might be lost," Greta announced as she and Winnie took the visitor chairs in front of Scarlett's desk. "Considering the way the man traveled the world—by boat, by train, on horseback—it becomes easier to believe manuscripts were misplaced and might be found."

"Worth a lot too," Winnie said.

"Anyone who found one might want the money and the fame," Greta agreed. "At least the money. That could go for Quartz or Tamsin."

"Sophie, Adam, or Rylla too," Scarlett said. "I can't imagine a farmer, a farmhand, or a student artist who couldn't use a windfall."

"I'll write up my notes and send them to everyone," Greta said. "Including Nina and Andy."

"Rylla's sketching in the gallery again, in case you're interested," Winnie said. Then, as she and Greta stood to go, she added, "I'd be interested to know how many murderers are motivated by greed."

The two left, Greta protesting Winnie's wording and Winnie apologizing profusely.

Scarlett sank back into her chair and did a bit more research—on birds with green, purple, and blue plumage. Armed with new information, she went to find Rylla. Scarlett was glad to see that Rylla wore her beanie, rather than the fishing hat, and there were no feathers in sight.

"Hello, Rylla. Two words for you. Green jay."

"Oh, you smartie. You've learned a new bird." Rylla continued sketching. "But you're wrong. Green jays live in Central America."

"Is your favorite a North American bird?"

"I'll do you one better. They're found in California."

"Cool. Hey, will you take me birding someday?"

Rylla cocked her head, reminding Scarlett of a bird again. "I was going to complain about the museum closing early on Fridays, but how about a trade instead? I won't complain if you come birding with me. Now."

"Now?"

"You have a lunch hour, don't you?"

"Can we keep it to an hour?" Scarlett asked.

"If we have to."

"Okay. Deal."

"Good." Rylla started packing up her gear. "Meet you out front in ten. You can drive. My car's low on gas."

Before Scarlett pulled out of the parking lot, she took out her phone and asked Rylla where they were headed.

"The estuary south of town. You won't need GPS."

"I'm letting the staff know where I'll be and when I'll be back." Scarlett glanced at her feet. "Is it marshy?"

"Your shoes will be fine. There's a boardwalk. Take a right out of the parking lot."

Rylla directed Scarlett all the way to a small gravel parking lot with a sign giving the estuary boardwalk's hours as dawn to dusk. Scarlett's was the lone car. Rylla slung a pair of binoculars around her neck, hopped out, and headed for a wide, well-kept trail into an area of tall reeds and marsh grasses.

"Boardwalk is this way," Rylla called.

Scarlett, thinking about the number of things that tall grasses could hide, hurried to catch up. "What kinds of birds will we see?"

"Plovers, dunlins, sanderlings, willets, American avocets, long-billed curlews, and marbled godwits. And a few others. But none if we talk too much."

They reached the boardwalk, and Scarlett was glad to see that it appeared to be new, solid, dry, and at least a foot above any quicksand that might be lurking nearby. The boardwalk took a curving path through the marsh, eventually leading them to a viewing platform, several feet higher than the boardwalk, up ahead of them. They climbed the steps to the platform, and Scarlett took in the view. More tall reeds and grasses were interrupted by areas of shallow water and mudflats.

Rylla set the lens cap from the binoculars on the railing and propped her elbows beside it.

"Let me know if you see a godwit," Scarlett said. "I like that name."

"Then keep an eye out for a sandpiper with a beak so long the poor thing should worry about tripping over it."

"You know what I worry about? Quartz. That he's someplace like this, hurt or sick, and not able to get help."

Rylla, who'd been pivoting as she surveyed the marsh, froze.

"What did you and Quartz argue about the night he disappeared?"

"How do you know about that?" Rylla asked.

"I don't know much about birds, but I do know how to—"

"Snoop?"

"Search for answers."

Rylla lowered the binoculars and peered at Scarlett. "With your suspicions, you aren't worried about being out here alone with me?"

"People know where we are, and that we came here together. If you go back to town alone, there are plenty of questions you'd have to answer." Scarlett shrugged. "And I'm bigger than you."

"Like that would make a difference if I hit you in the head. Like this." Rylla mimed swinging the binoculars at Scarlett. In doing so, she sent the lens cap flying. It landed in the mud a few yards from the platform. Rylla made a disgusted noise, sat down, and took off her shoes and socks.

"You can't go out there," Scarlett said.

"Why not?" Rylla rolled up her pant legs, ducked under the railing, and plopped into shallow water.

The horror of Scarlett's nightmare took her breath away. "What about quicksand?"

"There's no quicksand around here." Rylla picked her way through water and mud to the lens cap, raised it triumphantly, and started back.

Scarlett felt able to breathe again. Until she realized Rylla had stopped a few feet short of the platform. Then she heard a dry rattle from beneath her feet. "What was that?"

"It's watching me." Rylla's voice stretched thin, tight. "Coiled, rattling, and watching me."

"A rattlesnake? Back away from it."

"Snakes."

"More than one? Are you kidding?" *She has to be kidding.*

Rylla didn't answer.

"Back away," Scarlett repeated. *Why is she just standing there?* "Go sideways. Get away from them."

Tears streamed down Rylla's face. She remained rigid, silent.

This better not be a trap. But the silent tears convinced Scarlett it was all too real. She eyed the mud and took a shuddering breath. "Rylla, I'm coming to get you."

12

Scarlett left the viewing platform and moved several yards down the boardwalk. Questioning her sanity, she took off her shoes and socks, then rolled her pant legs to her knees. She took another shuddering breath then stepped into marsh, sinking up to her ankles in cold water, mud, and who knew what else underfoot.

Stifling a scream with every squelching step, she walked out into the marsh. Her path took her farther from the safety of the boardwalk than she liked, but it also kept her well away from Rylla's snakes and whatever friends they had rattling under the platform. Picturing other biting, bloodsucking, slithering, creatures circling her ankles and salivating over her toes, she walked slowly, carefully until she was behind Rylla.

As Rylla said, there were the snakes. Two of them, coiled on the concrete foundation of the platform, in a petrifying staring contest with Rylla.

"I'm here, Rylla," Scarlett said quietly, trying to keep her voice calm. She wanted Rylla to hear her, to know she was there before she touched her, so she didn't scare the rest of the daylights out of her. If Rylla jumped and startled the snakes, they were likely to strike. "I'm behind you. I'm going to put my hands on your shoulders, and we're going to move backward. We'll back away, then walk sideways, to our right, and then we'll get back up on the boardwalk. Okay? Here we go."

Scarlett had to give a couple of tugs before Rylla's rigid muscles relaxed enough that she could move away from the platform and the snakes.

When the women climbed back up onto the boardwalk, Scarlett offered a silent prayer of thanks and gave Rylla a quick hug.

Rylla shook Scarlett off. "I wasn't crying."

"And I wasn't screaming," Scarlett said with a shaky laugh.

"I mean I wasn't crying that night when I left Quartz."

"Oh. Did someone say you were?"

"He did. He was nothing but an old meddler. He told me I should tell Adam how I felt about him. I knew better, but I let him convince me. So then I did. I told Adam."

Scarlett wanted to call Rylla out for lying about knowing Adam, but she couldn't risk losing the chance to hear Rylla's unguarded story.

"When I talked to Adam, he couldn't have dumped me faster if I'd been a basket of rattlesnakes. That's what I was telling Quartz on Monday night. I was blaming him. Yelling at him for giving me bad advice." Rylla stomped back to the platform to get her shoes and socks.

Scarlett followed. "Did you tell this to the police?"

"I told them every nasty thing I said to him. I told him, 'Get out of my life. Leave me alone. Drop dead.'"

"Did you mean any of that?" Scarlett asked.

"He's gone, isn't he?"

"The police haven't arrested you."

"That's not my fault. You know what else isn't my fault? That the coast guard isn't hunting for drowned bodies. Are you afraid to give me a ride back to the museum?"

"Should I be?"

"If you weren't afraid of rattlesnakes, I guess not."

Rylla said nothing more on the ride back to the museum, or when Scarlett asked if she was all right to drive home. Scarlett watched her drive out of the parking lot, then she reentered the museum through the loading dock. Though she and Rylla had used bottles of water to rinse their feet so they could put their shoes and socks back on, she wanted to give hers a good wash. As she headed for a workroom with a utility sink, Winnie popped her head out of the security office.

"Is everything okay? You look rattled on the surveillance cameras."

"Follow me." Scarlett nodded toward the workroom. While she washed her feet in the deep sink, she told Winnie about her lunch hour adventure.

Winnie leaned back against one of the worktables in the room. When Scarlett got to the part about the rattlesnakes, she glanced over and saw Winnie pull her feet up and sit cross-legged on the table.

"There are no rattlesnakes in here, Winnie."

"But as you noticed, snakes make some people *hiss-terical*."

"Very punny, but fair enough." Scarlett related Rylla's story of her relationship with Adam and the argument with Quartz. "I'm not sure her description of the relationship adds up. It doesn't mesh with Sophie's." Scarlett dried her feet and put her shoes and socks back on.

Winnie returned her feet to the floor. "Sophie might've misread the relationship. She doesn't sound particularly warm or fuzzy, and might not recognize either true love or troubled love when she sees it."

"True," Scarlett said. "Or maybe Rylla's the young woman who showed up at the farm and annoyed Sophie. Then Sophie chewed Adam out and things went south with Rylla."

"So many possibilities when it comes to star-crossed romance," Winnie said. "Rylla might have lied about why she got mad at Quartz too. Whatever the story is, if Rylla believes it, she'll tell it convincingly."

"She was pretty convincing," Scarlett said. "Apparently rattlesnakes have a way of jolting people and getting them to open up."

"I admire rattlesnakes for that," Winnie said, "and I admire your skill at saving people from rattlesnakes."

"I might still be in shock."

"I'm glad to hear that, because what you did was definitely foolish. Going with her alone, walking through mud full of goodness-knows-what, and getting anywhere near the snakes."

"A lunch-hour birding trip shouldn't have been the proverbial basement no savvy sleuth goes into." Scarlett shuddered. "When she froze like that, all I could think of was Quartz alone somewhere. With snakes. You would have gone in after her too, Winnie. I know you well enough to know that about you."

"I hope I would, foolish or not," Winnie said. "As for Rylla's story, we have to keep in mind that we might not recognize what's genuine when it comes to someone we don't really know."

Back in her office, Scarlett called Officer Garcia to give her an update. Perhaps she would also hear one, but remembering Henry's complaint that morning about police reticence concerning the case, she thought better of starting with that request. "Hey, Nina. Is this a bad time?"

"You're fine," Nina said. "What have you got?"

Scarlett recounted the birding trip again, getting as far as the snakes before Nina cut in.

"We don't usually arrest snakes in their natural habitats. I'm not one to shoot them on sight either."

"I'm glad," Scarlett said.

"They aren't unheard of near the shore, but you're more likely to find them in wooded and rocky areas. They're shy, so you should feel honored."

"I'll work on that," Scarlett said. "Rylla's worried that she's responsible for Quartz's disappearance because of the things she yelled at him."

"Rylla might have an exaggerated idea of her impact on Quartz's actions and behavior."

"She's young," Scarlett said. "She has the exaggerated emotions to prove it."

"I remember being that age. I was ten feet tall and able to read people's minds with a single leap. I knew what lay in their hearts, whether good or bad."

Scarlett tried a more direct line. "Nina, I know you can't tell me what Rylla told you, but she's afraid her worries are being dismissed. She's afraid the coast guard isn't searching for a drowned body."

"Are you worried about that too?"

"I'm worried about everything to do with this disappearance."

"Some of what Rylla believes about her argument with Quartz might be true," Nina said. "We don't know. We're still working on it. But like I said, I do remember being her age. I outgrew most of it. I can assure you we're doing everything we can to find Quartz. We've had leads, tips, sightings. We've followed up on every one of them. None of them have panned out."

"You mean yet?"

"Sure. Yet."

After their call ended, Scarlett spent the next hour going over budget figures. She felt blessed to work for such an unusual museum. Thanks to its founder and benefactor, the Reed had no worries about funding. But the numbers weren't engrossing enough to keep her thoughts from wandering back to the missing man. She'd told Nina the truth when she'd said she worried about everything to do with Quartz's disappearance. Those worries included the hint of dejection she'd detected in Nina's usually positive attitude. Maybe a dose of Allie's coffee and her smiling face would be an antidote. Scarlett headed downstairs.

"Winnie told me you're a bona fide snake charmer," Allie said, handing Scarlett the coffee. "Did you really sling Rylla over your shoulder and carry her a mile through waist-deep mud?"

Scarlett laughed. "Then I went back for the snakes, draped them around my neck, nestled their seventeen babies in my pockets, and found that cute little family a new home farther from the beaten path."

Allie eyed her with open suspicion. "Some of Quartz's storytelling might have rubbed off on you. Do you know that guy talking to Winnie at the door?"

Scarlett turned and squinted her eyes to get a better look. A fifty-something man spoke at length to Winnie, who listened with her hands clasped behind her. Her sleek ponytail bobbed as she nodded.

"I don't recognize him," Scarlett said.

"He's got his phone out and here he comes with Winnie," Allie said. "Act casual."

Scarlett pasted on a large smile to greet Winnie and the visitor.

"Hi Greta," the visitor said into the phone. "I couldn't stand it another minute. I arranged for my graduate assistant to cover my classes and here I am. Yes, in Crescent Harbor. At the Reed."

"Henry?" Scarlett whispered. Winnie nodded. "Are Greta and Hal still here?"

"Yep." Allie pointed to the Barons hurrying toward them.

Henry Lang greeted his surprised friends with a hug for Greta and back slaps with Hal. "This is the only place I find you two when I call, so I came here first," he said after they'd expressed their astonishment at his arrival. "I appreciate you trying to temper my impatience, Hal, but I intend to use it. Historians are detectives, and I'm here to help find Quartz."

"That sounds like exactly what we need right now," Greta said.

"I have a motel room," Henry said. "So I won't be a bother to anyone. Quartz and I explored a few old mines together. Spelunked a time or two, as well. I know how to read maps and find my way with a compass."

He didn't strike Scarlett as a man ready to go anywhere with a compass. As he absently scratched his well-padded stomach, she wondered how many years it had been since he'd done anything like explore or spelunk. Judging by his figure, he was used to a sedentary life.

"Where do you plan to start?" Greta asked. "Solo exploring might not be the best plan."

"Research first," Henry said. "Plans to follow."

"Would Quartz actually have risked going somewhere dangerous alone?" Hal asked.

"If he thought he knew what he was getting into, I think he might. I feel responsible." Henry closed his eyes and brought clasped hands to his lips. "I took him out to celebrate when he told me about the equipment he'd discovered, free for the hauling. I encouraged him to come here and get it. Made the arrangements for him to stay with you. Gave him money for gas."

"Is he really that hard up?" Greta asked.

"You've seen the state of his truck. I even tried to rent something more reliable for him. He's stuck in his ways."

"The truck is still in front of their house," Scarlett said.

"Has anyone checked to see if he rented another vehicle?" Henry asked. "Do we know if the police checked?"

"The answer to your first question is no and the second is we don't know. We don't, do we?" Hal asked the others, who shook their heads.

"That's where I'll start, then," Henry said. "There can't be that many car rental firms in the area, but if there are, I have my work cut out for me."

"We," Hal said. "I'll come with you."

The Reed closed to the public at two o'clock on Fridays, but Scarlett often stayed later to work in the quiet when there were few interruptions. It had been tempting to join Hal and Henry or to split the list if there were many rental agencies in the area. She had faith, though, that the police had already canvassed those businesses. No, after her lunchtime adventure, attention to her own profession—even research into art of the Black Death—felt cozy.

Besides, Scarlett had another mystery to solve.

She settled into her office chair. With a mellow cello concerto playing in the background, she did a search for Tamsin—and hit a brick wall with her first attempt. The University of Edinburgh did not open its student directory to the public.

"As it should be," Scarlett said, moving on to social media, where she found plenty.

Tamsin had a solid social media presence with posts and photographs backing up her graduate student status. Her posts and pictures showed her at work at an antiquarian bookshop in Edinburgh. The shop, with a façade that immediately made Scarlett want to book a flight, specialized in rare editions and ephemera of Scots writers, notably those of James M. Barrie, Sir Walter Scott, and Robert Louis Stevenson. Scarlett clicked on the link to the bookshop's website and found herself sighing over the adorable tartan-covered miniature books on the homepage. Her gaze stuck on the graphic below the miniatures. Made to look like an antique brass plaque, it read, *Rare volumes and ephemera handled with discretion.*

To Scarlett, that sounded an awful lot like "No questions asked."

13

"Dead end at the car rental agencies," Hal said, staring into his coffee Saturday morning before the Reed opened. At an indrawn breath from Scarlett and a gentle cough from Greta, he raised his head. "What?"

"Poor choice of words, dear," Greta said. "'Dead end.'"

"My apologies." Hal threw back his head and shouted at the ceiling, "'O dolt! As ignorant as dirt!' More lines from *Othello*, by the way. That play's a gold mine for useful lines. And ignorant is exactly what Henry and I were, thinking we could waltz into rental agencies and they would happily share their customer information with us."

"I ran into the same problem trying to access the University of Edinburgh's student directory," Scarlett said.

"Times and privacy policies have changed," Greta agreed.

"But wouldn't it be nice if everyone made exceptions for amateur sleuths?" Allie asked.

"Which is why I say thank goodness for social media." Scarlett told them what she'd learned online about Tamsin.

"Remind me to be more careful about anything I post," Allie said.

"Ditto," Scarlett said. "Of course, Tamsin's job at the bookseller doesn't prove she's here doing anything other than research for her degree. And 'rare volumes and ephemera handled with discretion' doesn't necessarily mean the shop deals with ill-gotten books or manuscripts."

"But you sent the information to Nina?" Greta asked.

"Yes."

"And we'll add it to our growing accumulation of 'everything helps,'" Greta said.

"How'd Henry handle getting nothing from the rental agencies?" Allie asked.

"Between that and none of us knowing what happened to Quartz's package, I thought he might break down and weep," Hal said. "He'd make a great photographic study for you, Allie. So expressive."

"He exhibits his intellect and his impatience in every question, every inflection," Greta said. "I expect him to start tearing at his hair anytime."

"If he had any left to tear at," Hal added.

"What are his plans for today?" Scarlett asked.

"He said he'd stop by and let us know." Greta put her arm through Hal's. "I almost wish he hadn't come down here. The worry and frustration are magnified up close like this. It's a selfish wish, though. He's added another layer to my worries, and that's not what I should be focused on."

"Bring him by my office when he gets here," Scarlett said. "Maybe seeing again that we're all concerned will help. Maybe helping to alleviate his angst will help you too."

An hour later, a knock on Scarlett's open office door pulled her attention from a draft of the museum's newsletter. Greta had taken her up on the offer to stop by with Henry.

"Come sit down, you two. Good to see you, Henry." Scarlett didn't ask how he'd slept. The dark circles under his eyes told her everything she needed to know. She came from behind her desk and joined them in the visitor chairs.

"Henry decided to approach the search for Quartz the way he approaches his professional research." Greta sounded upbeat, but her expression included a shadow of doubt.

"I'll avoid the baggage of other people's conclusions," Henry said, "starting fresh with primary sources."

"You don't want us to loop you in with what we've already done?" Scarlett asked.

Henry waved the offer away. "Not that I don't value your work, but I prefer to follow my own methods. If I reach the same conclusions you have, the case will be that much stronger."

"How will you identify your primary sources?" Scarlett asked. Out of the corner of her eye she saw Greta mouth *thank you*.

"I can use your help there," Henry admitted. "I want to start by talking to people Quartz talked to."

"One of them is here now," Greta said. "A young woman named Rylla Summerville. She's an art student, and she's sketching in the gallery as we speak."

Henry's reaction tickled Scarlett. *Deer in the headlights*, she thought. *No, a teddy bear in the headlights.*

"Ah, hmm, may I ask a favor then? Will you come with me? I don't want to intimidate her."

Scarlett barely suppressed a chuckle as she and Greta took Henry to meet Rylla. He was about as far from intimidating as anyone could get.

Rylla made brief eye contact when Greta introduced Henry as a friend of Quartz's. Hatless for a change, she ran a hand over her feather-patterned hair, then signed her drawing with a flourish.

"Excuse me," Henry said, "but your hair is quite striking."

"Thanks. I prefer 'perfect.'"

Greta studied Rylla's work. "This is very good, Rylla. But you've signed it Beryl Summerville."

"My given name, after my grandmother. She'd probably think my hair is perfect."

"Hasn't she seen it?" Henry asked.

"She died before I was born. So I don't really know if she was cool or if she'd say my hair is perfect. But she loved and painted birds. She was named for Beryl Markham."

"Beryl Markham was an aviator who flew like a bird," Greta said. "If your grandmother was named for her, liked birds, and painted, I guarantee she was cool."

"Thought so," Rylla said. "Beryl's a stone too."

"You have been talking to Quartz," Henry said. "What else did he say?"

"Beryl is supposed to help you find lost property."

"And now he's lost," Henry said. "Do you know who else he talked to? Where he went?"

Rylla shrugged. "Left Field Farm. I saw him there Monday when I was plein air painting." She dropped her gaze. "I didn't have permission, so I don't like spreading the news around."

"What was Quartz doing at this farm?" Henry asked.

"I can't tell you for sure, but if I had to guess, he was being told to leave," Rylla said. "Sophie's kind of hospitality encourages people to leave. And to paint without permission."

"Were you there Tuesday afternoon?" Scarlett asked.

"The day after Quartz disappeared?" Rylla asked. "That's the day you took Tamsin out there, isn't it? Have you seen much of her lately?"

"Not since Thursday."

"That doesn't make you curious? But no, I wasn't painting there Tuesday."

But she'd rushed off somewhere Tuesday morning. And Adam hadn't been at work.

Henry followed Scarlett and Greta from the gallery. "I'm going to take my thoughts for a walk through the other galleries. Draw my own conclusions."

"Join us for lunch later, if you like," Greta said.

Henry nodded and paced away with his hands clasped behind him.

Greta turned to Scarlett. "Can we believe Rylla?"

"If she isn't lying now, then she did initially. About not knowing Adam or anything about the farm. But I had no trouble believing her yesterday in the marsh. Call it trial by rattlesnake."

"Why lie in the first place?" Greta asked. "No, forget I asked. How long did I teach? For as many years as there are reasons for lying."

"Fear being a big one," Scarlett said.

"And not every twenty-year-old is a kid, but they aren't all adults either." Greta put a hand on Scarlett's arm. "Here's a more pressing question. It's been stirring in the back of my mind, but Rylla brought it charging to the front. Where's Tamsin?"

"Busy with research. Buying and setting up a new laptop. We saw her two days ago, and she has no particular reason to hang out at the Reed."

"But if she's after a valuable manuscript and if that's what Quartz was investigating as well? Scarlett, what if she's missing too?"

"Rylla implied as much. So is she worried about Tamsin or—"

"Or giving hints?" Greta asked.

"I'll call Nina."

Luke improved Scarlett's spirits by stopping by unexpectedly with carryout from The Salty Dog shortly before the museum closed at noon. "California clubs," he said. "Fresh vegetables, turkey breast, crispy bacon, and house-special aioli on dark sourdough rye with herbs."

"Eat in the garden?" Scarlett asked.

"We're on the same wavelength."

They stopped by the coffee shop to pick up drinks before Allie closed and ran into Henry waiting for Greta and Hal. Scarlett made introductions. "Henry, I'd like you to meet Luke Anderson. Luke, this is Quartz's good friend Henry Lang."

"I'm sorry about the reason for your visit," Luke said.

"I'm feeling quite lost myself," Henry said. "Are you part of this amateur sleuth group?"

"I do what I can." Luke caught Scarlett's eye with a silent question in his. *Does he know I'm with the FBI?*

Scarlett gave a minimal head shake. If Luke wanted to introduce himself as an agent, that was up to him.

"The police better be doing all they can," Henry said.

"I guarantee they are," Allie said.

"Forgive me. I didn't mean to disparage the force." Henry scrubbed a hand over his face. "I'm on edge, tired, because of—well, all of it. And especially because I'm not used to the adrenaline I've been living on."

"You should try to get a nap in this afternoon," Scarlett said.

"First I want to walk around town." Henry indicated the bag Luke held. "Eat at The Salty Dog. See Crescent Harbor through Quartz's eyes. A question for you, Scarlett. Are you investigating this Tamsin woman?"

"Yes."

"Good. Don't elaborate. I have my own methods, you see," Henry said to Luke. "Operating with a blank slate."

"I can see that being a useful technique," Luke said.

"Hal offered to be my guide this afternoon, but I made him promise to show only. No telling. He didn't think we should make the trip to the farm Beryl mentioned. I might do that on my own tomorrow."

"Beryl?" Luke and Allie asked.

"Rylla's given name," Scarlett said.

"Hal's also going to show me around the Greek to Me Theater. As a treat," Henry said. "To give my mind a break."

"After the playhouse, maybe you should kick back on the beach for a while," Allie said. "There's nothing better for letting go of stress."

"If it isn't crowded, I might. Then it's back to the motel to crash."

***

Over their lunch in the museum garden, Scarlett brought Luke up to date. "So we're suspicious of Tamsin and worried about her at the same time, and now we have Henry wandering around treating this like an academic exercise. What if he gets into trouble?"

"What if he *causes* trouble?" Luke said. "You know, there's an old FBI saying that too many amateur sleuths confuse the plot."

Scarlett frowned. "Do you think the rest of us should back off?"

"Has Nina suggested that?"

"No."

"Then I'd say you've earned the police department's trust. You, Allie, Greta, Hal, Winnie—together you're a known variable. But too great a quantity of people poking around can be an issue."

"But the more people who know Quartz is missing, the more will be on the lookout for him."

"That's the balancing act," Luke said. "Shall we go to church and the farmers market tomorrow? Give you a break from all this?"

Scarlett nodded reluctantly. Until they found Quartz, a break was the last thing she wanted.

The Crescent Harbor Library struck Scarlett as a building lost in thought as she approached it that afternoon. Housed in the former Santa Catalina Mission, the soaring facade of pale adobe had a few windows high up, like eyes half-closed and contemplating the sky. Librarian Maria Huerta, on the other hand, had flashing eyes and a curious mind that took in everything around her and much else besides. She knew all the scandals in Crescent Harbor as well as the history—and Scarlett could go for a little of each. Sophie hadn't told her about Quartz's visit to the farm, and Scarlett was interested in what else she might be hiding.

"Scarlett," Maria greeted her. "One of my favorite patrons."

"Isn't every patron one of your favorites?"

"Of course. What can I do for you?"

"I hope you can give me a bit of information."

"Book talk first. Need a recommendation?"

"Sure."

"Go retro. Take home some Dorothy L. Sayers. Her mysteries are excellent, a perfect mixture of clever lightened with humor. And her main sleuth, Lord Peter, is dashing, charming, and brilliant. Now, what kind of information do you need?"

"More like scuttlebutt."

"That's often the best information."

Scarlett lowered her voice. "Sophie Morata. What's her story? For a businesswoman, she's—"

"As customer-friendly as a cactus? Well, who can blame her? Her husband took off. Left her and the farm in financial straits. She's worked hard to make that farm pay, but she's guarded the land and her privacy ever since."

"Was it a scandal when he left?"

"The scandal was why she didn't get rid of him sooner."

"Get rid of him?"

Maria's eyes widened at the echo of her words. "I should've said 'sent him packing.' The other way sounds rather dark, doesn't it?"

"What made him such a bad guy that she would have sent him packing?"

"He just wasn't a nice person. To anyone."

Scarlett considered that must have made them a good match, but kept her observation to herself. "When was that, and what was his name?"

"Decades ago. As for his name—wow, let me think." Maria bowed her head and tented her fingers. Scarlett felt as if she were watching a living computer process a request. "Engler. Billy Engler. And he left the year my son, Javi's, soccer team won a championship. That makes it twenty-three years ago. In March, I believe. Is this about finding Mr. Sutton?"

Scarlett nodded.

"He's in my prayers."

"Thanks, Maria."

Scarlett went to find back issues of the *Rip Current News* in the stacks. Many residents joked that the local paper contained more gossip than news. Scarlett didn't always appreciate the stories in the *Current* either. Particularly in situations like this.

She sat down at a table with issues for the year leading up to the month Billy Engler left the area, skimming for reports of police calls to Left Field Farm. She didn't find any, but knew that didn't mean all had been well there. Scanning for the farm's name, she found ads for produce but nothing more. She had no luck looking through papers two and three years before Billy Engler had disappeared.

Not willing to give up on the *Rip Current News* yet, she decided to search for Adam Gray—the Gray Ghost. Nina had said he'd played high school football a decade before. Scarlett brought the relevant issues to her study table and was quickly rewarded. The paper feted the Gray Ghost in an October issue as Crescent Harbor High's Football Player of the Year. She enjoyed following him through the football season and into baseball, at which he also excelled. Sadly, the paper shamed him shortly after graduation. He and a group of environmentalists were arrested for protesting new construction near the beach. Below that article, she recognized someone staring at her from the police reports—Virgil Soto.

Virgil had been arrested for burglary. *Virgil?* Scarlett sat momentarily stunned. Then she searched for articles telling the rest of the story. She found one, with the district attorney dropping charges while expressing frustration. Scarlett knew the feeling.

Scarlett made copies of the articles about Adam and Virgil. She went to see what Maria knew about Virgil, but the head librarian had gone home early.

Scarlett left the library more puzzled than ever. What was Sophie's story? Scarlett could understand a wish for privacy, but would Sophie continue to guard that privacy, her past, and her land so closely if that meant someone else—like Quartz—had no future?

14

Cleo watched from the back of the sofa as Scarlett paced the living room with her phone pressed to her ear. "Nina, hi. It's your favorite pest. Have you got a minute?"

"You sound out of breath. Everything okay?"

"Fine. I walked home from the library. And I'm pacing now." Scarlett flopped onto the sofa.

"Well, you are my favorite pest, so go ahead."

"Did you know Virgil Soto was arrested for burglary?"

"What?" A sound like a chair's front legs slamming to the floor followed Nina's exclamation. "When? I haven't heard anything about it."

"That's because it was ten years ago. I read it in a back issue of the *Rip Current News*."

"Oh for goodness' sake, Scarlett. Current issues of the *Current* are dangerous enough."

"So you knew about the old case?"

"Actually, no. That would've been before my time in the department, but you'd think it might have come up with this case."

"Not necessarily," Scarlett said. "The charges were dropped. But that's what has me puzzled. The article about the DA dropping the charges said he was frustrated, but it didn't say Virgil was innocent. So what does that mean?"

"It might mean he was innocent. It might mean they didn't have enough evidence to convict."

"Does it bear investigating?"

"Everything does," Nina said.

"Okay, so then here's some other old news." Scarlett told her about Adam Gray's brush with the law. "He was barely out of high school, though, and you told Winnie he hasn't had any legal troubles." Scarlett waited through a moment of silence on Nina's end. "Sorry, at this point, I realize I'm dropping an awful lot of 'everything' in your lap."

"No, you're fine," Nina said, sounding preoccupied. "I'm logging into a database to search for both cases. Anything else in the *Rip Current*'s treasure trove?"

"No. In fact, I didn't even find what I was looking for."

"That doesn't mean it doesn't exist," Nina said.

"I know."

"And just because we haven't found Quartz doesn't mean we won't."

"I know that too."

"Reaching for answers is fine, Scarlett, but be careful. In everyday life, reaching too far can lead to a fall. You had your brush with snakes yesterday. I don't want anything happening to my favorite pest, okay? Talk to you later."

Scarlett disconnected and found that Cleo had twisted herself like a pretzel so that she gazed at Scarlett upside down.

"That perspective probably makes more sense for this case than viewing it right side up." She scratched Cleo's chin until the cat purred. "What does this do for you, huh?"

Scarlett rubbed her own chin. "No. Not helping. Where is this all going, Cleo? We keep saying that everything helps, but if we collect many more bits and pieces of information that might or might not be facts, we'll be buried alive." Scarlett drew in a sharp breath. *Erase that last thought*, she told herself and jumped up to start pacing again.

"I'm feeling like Henry. Impatient. I need to do something."

She pulled her phone out and tapped on Greta's number. "Hey, Greta, are Hal and Henry still out and about?"

"Indeed they are," Greta said. "Hal's keeping me updated on their progress around town. They're at The Vintage Idiot, and I think they'll be there for a while. Hal says Henry is in love, but he's not sure whether it's with Danielle or the shop. Maybe both."

"Henry and Danielle would make an interesting couple. How do you feel about going on a fact-finding mission of our own?"

"Can we do it without crossing paths with Hal and Henry?" Greta asked. "They're enjoying themselves, and I wouldn't want them to think we're checking up on them."

"Have they changed their minds about going to Left Field Farm?"

"No. Next on their list is Greek to Me," Greta said.

"Good. I want to give Sophie a chance to tell us that Quartz visited the farm. Or to tell us why, on Tuesday, when I described him, she acted as though she'd never seen him."

Greta was quiet for a moment before saying, "That sounds like a confrontation, Scarlett."

"We'll try to keep it from being one. I'm not big on confrontations."

"Neither am I."

"There is more I'd like to ask her," Scarlett said. "I'll tell you about it on the way out."

"In that case, you talk and I'll drive. I'll pick you up in a few minutes."

Greta was as good as her word. Within minutes Scarlett was buckling herself into Greta's Buick Encore. As Greta drove, Scarlett told her what she'd heard from Maria, and what she had and hadn't found in the *Rip Current News*.

"Maria certainly has her ear to the ground," Greta said. "I don't remember hearing anything about Sophie having a husband in the first place, much less that he left her. And the name Billy Engler rings no bells."

"This happened before you retired. You would have been focused on your students and your research."

"But another missing man?" Greta asked. "What do we know about this Billy Engler?"

"Only what Maria said, that Sophie should've tossed him out sooner."

"And what about Tamsin? Is she missing? You called Nina. Has she let you know anything?"

"No."

"I'm sorry, Scarlett. This is upsetting. I need to pull over." Greta steered into the parking lot of Rosita's, Scarlett's favorite Mexican restaurant, and shut off the engine.

Scarlett put a hand on Greta's arm. "We don't have to do this."

"I think we do," Greta said. "We'll figure out our approach. I'll focus on that and I'll be fine. Now, asking about Quartz is one thing, but bringing up abandonment by a possibly abusive husband—"

"Let's leave out the abusive part. That's nothing more than a guess on my part."

"An informed guess," Greta said. "Maria's information is usually spot-on."

"Let's focus on Quartz for now," Scarlett said. "Sophie lied about him being there, even if it was a lie by omission. We need to know why."

"Hal and I have always believed that when a child has done something wrong or by mistake, and the parents know, it's better for the parents to say they know. Don't invite a lie by asking."

"That might be the way to approach Sophie about Quartz."

Greta made calming motions with both hands, as though quelling a crowd—or her own worries. "We'll be matter-of-fact, forthright, and calm. We'll say we have it on good authority that Quartz visited Left Field."

Scarlett nodded. "Emphasize that we want to find him, to help him. We'll ask for her story. Be a sympathetic audience."

"Voices modulated, expressions and body language relaxed," Greta said. "Keep accusations out of it."

"I can try to do that," Scarlett said. Then she corrected herself. "No, there is no try. I will do that. Cleo could help model the correct behavior. She'd recommend rolling over and baring our throats."

"Except that we don't want to roll over. We want information," Greta said. "One more thing before we're on our way. What if Adam Gray is there? We don't know much about him, but shouldn't we be prepared with questions for him?"

Scarlett smacked herself in the forehead. "I hadn't even thought about running into him. But yes, you're right. Hang on." From her purse, she took the newspaper articles she'd printed at the library. She handed the articles about Adam to Greta. "Here's a little background. If Rylla is to be believed, she and he used to be an item. Maybe Rylla had a chance to introduce Adam to Quartz."

Greta tapped the front-page picture of Adam as the football player of the year. "I recognize him from the college. If I remember right, he was popular and had a certain reputation."

"For what?"

"That I don't remember. I only heard about it secondhand." Greta's face lit up. "From a colleague I've been meaning to call." She pulled out her phone. "She can be a chatterbox, but now is the perfect time to hear everything she has to say."

Scarlett, afraid the call might turn into a prolonged reminiscence, wasn't so sure it was the perfect time. But once they had gotten the information they needed, Greta suggested lunch toward the end of the week and a chance to really catch up on everything else.

"That was instructive," Greta said after disconnecting. "Adam was a horticultural student. His reputation was for a thumb so green it glowed."

"That sounds like a good thing, especially for Sophie and Left Field Farm."

"Yes, if he confines himself to working on legal plants. He and his thumb propagated Yadon's rein orchid, an endangered species native to Monterey County," Greta said.

"Why would that be illegal?" Scarlett asked. "I would have thought it would be in the ecosystem's best interest to increase the number of plants in an endangered species."

"I can see where you'd think that, but you have to acquire the plants legally. There were questions about where he got the ones he used. He was questioned several times by the department head and agents from the California Department of Fish and Wildlife. He always managed to come out smelling like a rose."

"Nina says he's had no further legal problems," Scarlett said.

"Because he doesn't go to protests anymore, or because he's smart enough not to get caught?"

"She also cautioned me on the dangers of overreaching. I might be approaching that point here, but what if Quartz stumbled into something between Adam and Rylla involving illegally harvesting and selling rare orchids?"

"Rylla said Quartz encouraged her to make her feelings known to Adam. Would he do that if he'd stumbled into their black-market operation?"

"He might have stumbled after he encouraged her," Scarlett said. "Or maybe he didn't realize what he'd stumbled into before it was too late."

"Are we scaring ourselves?" Greta asked, then answered herself. "We're not. We're brainstorming." She started the engine, pulled around, and got back on the road. "And whatever storm we're kicking up, it's nothing compared to what Quartz must be weathering."

Sophie, wearing overalls and a frown, stood with her arms crossed as she watched Greta park in front of the farmhouse. "I don't sell to the public except at the farmers market," she said as Greta got out. "And if you're selling, then I don't want it."

"Hi, Sophie." Scarlett came around from the other side of the car. "We aren't buying or selling."

"We have information for you." Greta held out her hand. "Hi, Sophie. I'm Greta Baron."

"Your husband acts at the theater in Crescent Harbor."

"You've seen him?"

"He was good in *The Frogs*."

Greta laughed. "He'll be tickled to hear that."

"So, this information," Sophie said. "Is it the clichéd information that will be to my advantage?"

"Yes, and to the advantage of a friend of ours named Quartz Sutton." Scarlett found herself unexpectedly choking up.

Greta put her arm through Scarlett's.

Sophie said nothing aloud, but Scarlett saw plenty unspoken in her eyes.

"Before he went missing, Quartz was staying with Hal and me," Greta said. "He took us to dinner Monday night, then went for a walk on the beach. His belongings and his truck are still at our house, but there has been no sign of him since that evening."

"I haven't seen him," Sophie said, her voice rasping with worry—for Quartz, or for herself?

"But you did see him here sometime before Monday night," Scarlett said. "We simply want to know if he said anything that might shed light on what could have happened to him."

"He's an enthusiast for old mines," Greta said. "You have an old mine, which we know you warn people about. Is there any chance—"

"No. Not now. I never wanted any of this." Sophie's words became anguished. She wrapped her arms around herself as if holding in unbearable pain.

"Sophie, if something's happened, we know it's not your fault," Scarlett said.

"I don't know," Sophie said. "I don't. But I'm afraid."

"You should tell us," Greta said gently. "Maybe we can help."

"I think he fell down the mine."

Scarlett stopped breathing. She thought her heart might have stopped too.

"Quartz," Greta whispered.

Sophie shook her head. "Billy."

"Sorry?" Scarlett said.

"My rotten husband. I think he fell through the rotten flooring into the mine shaft."

"I thought he abandoned you," Scarlett said. "Twenty-three years ago."

"I thought he did too." Sophie drew in a shuddering breath. "He threatened to often enough. He never did follow through on much, so when he did go, I actually applauded. Then I felt ashamed." She took a bandanna from a pocket and blew her nose. "When I realized no one had heard from him in months and then years, I began to consider the possibility. A few years back, Adam found the mine opening with the broken floorboards. I thought about it again, but not enough to do anything."

"Except warn people away from the mine?" Scarlett said.

"Of course. I forbade Adam from exploring it further, and I'm absolutely certain your friend didn't go near it. All he asked about was Stevenson's camping trip, like your Scottish friend. I don't let anyone near the mine."

"It's good that you're trying to protect everyone. But you should call the police about your husband," Greta said. "Really."

Sophie drew in another shuddering breath and agreed.

"We didn't see Adam," Greta said on the way back to town.

"I don't mind," Scarlett said. "I feel as though I've been through the wringer. Imagine how Sophie feels. How could she hide that all these years? I guess it explains her antisocial nature. She must not have wanted to let anyone get too close to her for fear they'd guess the truth."

"Hmm," Greta said. "I know what Hal would say about her certainty that no one has been near the mine. He'd quote Hamlet. 'The lady doth protest too much, methinks.'"

"I got that impression too," Scarlett said. "She might genuinely think that Adam has gone along with her ban on exploring the mine. Like Nina is genuinely sure Adam hasn't had any legal troubles. Which he hasn't, officially."

"But not for lack of using his green thumb, at least while he was at the college."

"He might have skirted Sophie's intent," Scarlett said. "Maybe he didn't explore further. But did that stop him from showing the mine to Quartz?"

15

As soon as Greta dropped Scarlett off at home, Scarlett called Luke. "Hi, it's short notice," she said, unlocking her front door, "but Greta and I are hosting a get-together at my place this evening. We're calling it Sad Stories and Suspicions. Want to come?"

"Wow. Sounds suspenseful."

"All the cool sleuths will be here. We hope they will, anyway. Either way, there will be ice cream."

"What time?"

"Seven thirty for amateur sleuths. Six for professionals who'd like supper first."

"I love being special. See you at six."

"Great. Can you pick up ice cream on your way over?" Scarlett laughed at the sounds of mock outrage from Luke. "Sorry, Agent Anderson. Professional sleuths should see that kind of thing coming a mile away. By the way, do you think this ice cream-fueled sleuthing session will help?"

"It can't hurt," Luke said. "First of all, we might get somewhere with this puzzle. Second, I don't have to wait until tomorrow to see you again."

"I like those reasons. Plus ice cream."

Happy to hear his laugh, Scarlett hung up, then said to Cleo, "You get extra treats if you're a well-behaved friend of the sleuths this evening."

Cleo and Luke met the guests at the door as they arrived. Cleo rode in Luke's arms so that she was appropriately regal—and so she didn't slip out into the night.

Allie, last to arrive, leaned forward to touch noses with Cleo, then surveyed the others arranged around Scarlett's living room. "Is it lucky or sad that none of us had other plans on a Saturday night?" she asked.

"Well, you know what they say about dates," Winnie said. "Such an underrated fruit."

"I'm sitting next to Winnie," Hal said. "Because she's the most pun."

Winnie gave him a high five.

"Henry sends his regrets," Greta said. "He's gone back to his motel for an early night."

"How did it go for him this afternoon?" Luke asked.

"It went well, I think," Hal said. "The poor guy is taking this hard. I like his methodical approach, though."

"Didn't you say another word for it might be 'plodding'?" Greta asked with a wry smile.

"I did. But I can't deny that his method makes sense."

"I'm sorry he won't be here to add his thinking tonight," Scarlett said.

"Remember he likes to work with a blank slate," Hal said. "He felt good about what he saw, did, and learned today. He's systematic, and no dummy. He might actually come up with the answer to what's happened. In four or five months. And please don't ever tell him I said that."

"We each have our own ways of working," Scarlett said. "I'm just grateful that the six of us work so well together. And I know we've seen a lot of each other today, so thanks for coming over."

"How many days has Quartz been missing now?" Allie asked.

"Five," Winnie said.

"Then let's do what we can and reward ourselves with ice cream afterward," Greta said. "The ice cream will be a dry run for the ice cream party we'll throw for Quartz when we get him out of whatever fix he's in. Why don't you take over, Scarlett?" Greta squeezed in beside Hal on the sofa, and he put his arm around her.

Allie perched on a tall chair brought in from the kitchen, leaving the chairs on either side of the fireplace for Scarlett and Luke.

"Let's start with stories," Scarlett said. "We've been hearing a lot of them from Quartz, Sophie, Tamsin, Rylla, and even Henry."

"Reading them too," Luke added, "when you've sent us updates."

"I read one about Adam today in an old issue of the *Rip Current News*," Scarlett said.

"What about him?" Winnie asked.

"Nina was partially right when she told us he's had no legal troubles," Scarlett said. "But only if you modify that with 'recently.'" She told them about Adam's protest.

"Protesting construction near the beach? Sorry," Allie said, "that doesn't sound like enough to bring out the pitchforks."

"Greta has more," Scarlett said.

Greta relayed the phone call with her former colleague. "There's no proof he's continued working with these orchids—and by working, I mean illegally collecting and selling—but if he is, and Quartz learned of it, there's a possible motive for Quartz's disappearance."

"And how do we know Rylla told us the truth about why she was angry with Quartz in the surveillance footage?" Scarlett asked. "If she knows that Adam's up to something illegal, she might have been telling Quartz to butt out."

"Wow," Winnie said.

"It's all conjecture. We know that." Scarlett glanced at Luke.

"No complaints," Luke said. "They're solid conjectures."

"The main reason I don't like them is because they make it sound like Quartz won't be coming back," Allie said.

"You won't like our conjectures about Sophie any better," Greta said.

Scarlett told them Maria's story about how Sophie's marriage to Billy Engler had ended, and then Sophie's theory about what caused Billy's disappearance.

"If Sophie's been cavalier about one dead man," Greta said, "we have to ask if she'd care that much about a second one."

"I don't see that," Winnie said. "What's the connection between Sophie and Quartz?"

"He did go out to Left Field Farm," Scarlett said. "Tuesday, when I was out there with Tamsin, I described him to Sophie, and she didn't say anything about him being there. He and Tamsin both asked about the Robert Louis Stevenson camping story, but Sophie said nothing to confirm that until we confronted her today."

"Unlike Cleo," Hal said as Cleo leapt from the floor into his lap, "Sophie is known for being antisocial."

"And it's easy to pick on someone who's antisocial," Scarlett said. "I don't mean to do that. Cleo, don't pick on Hal just because he's as social as you are."

Cleo moved to Greta's lap.

Greta rubbed the cat's ears, bringing on a rumbling purr that Scarlett heard across the room.

"Putting aside how Quartz would have gotten to the farm without his truck," Greta said, "Sophie keeps bees. What if he was out there poking around for Stevenson's campsite, the mine, whatever. With or without permission. And what if he was stung by her bees and had a fatal reaction?"

"If he's allergic, wouldn't he be prepared?" Winnie asked. "I would be."

Allie shook her head. "Being prepared doesn't always cut it with beestings. And you might not be prepared if you don't know you're allergic."

But are you saying she then got rid of the body? Antisocial is one thing. Being so cold that you do something like that is another."

Scarlett considered that explanation. "The beehives aren't that close to the house. What if he was stung, had a reaction, and stumbled into the woods?"

"And if he was there without permission, no one would know to search for him," Winnie said. "That could have happened if we put aside the question of how he got out there. It also would clear up my question of why Sophie would tell you her husband might have been at the bottom of the mine for decades if she'd buried Quartz somewhere."

Luke shrugged. "The person Quartz waved to at the end of the surveillance video could have taken him out to the farm. As long as we're coming up with stories."

"That's a good one," Winnie said. "Good enough that I'm getting the creeps. What are we going to do with all our stories?"

Greta continued to scratch the cat's head. "Cleo seems to have an opinion. She's making unhappy noises at the front window."

"Probably at someone with the gall to walk a dog through her domain," Scarlett said. "Territorial much, Cleo?"

Winnie held up a hand. "Wait. Hush." The others quieted and Winnie cocked her head toward the window. "I don't think it's a dog," she whispered. "I think there's a prowler. Near the window. Listening."

"How do you hear someone listening?" Allie whispered back.

Luke, getting to his feet, spoke at normal volume. "Do we have all the stories? Is there more, Scarlett?" He moved quietly toward the door, making a rolling motion with his hand, encouraging her to carry on and try to behave normally.

Scarlett picked up on his cue. "There's the story behind the package. That's still pretty much a blank page."

Luke took a small flashlight from a pocket. Winnie stood, pulled out her phone, and tapped on the flashlight app. Luke put his hand on the doorknob and motioned for Scarlett to continue.

Scarlett nodded. "It's a shame that when the police had the package they didn't open—"

At that, Luke flicked on the flashlight, and in one fluid movement opened the door, stepped through, and aimed the light across the front of the house. Winnie followed, shining her phone toward the sidewalk and street.

"Allie, keep Cleo in, will you?" Scarlett stepped outside to see Luke and Winnie confer near the street, then split up and circle around to the back of the house. They returned soon enough, switching off their lights, and the three went back inside.

"Thanks, Allie." Scarlett took Cleo from her. "Where'd Greta and Hal go?"

"We're here," Greta called from the kitchen. "Dishing up the ice cream."

Hal brought in a tray with heaping bowls of salted caramel fudge ice cream. "We have more work ahead of us tonight, but after the excitement of our security expert and FBI agent rushing out into the night, we all need this."

"What did you find out there?" Allie asked.

"Someone was disappearing down the street when I opened the door," Luke said. "That could've been a legitimate, hurried walk."

"I don't think it was." Winnie took her ice cream and ate a spoonful. "Cleo doesn't either."

"Neither do I, really," Luke said. "We have no proof, though."

"How tall?" Allie asked. "Male or female?"

"Someone able to move quickly and easily," Luke said. "Too quickly. The shrubbery at the end of the block didn't help. The person was wearing a jacket that blew open so I couldn't see their shape.

Between five-six and five-ten at a rough estimate. That's all I got. It could've been anyone. Sorry."

"You're sorry?" Allie said. "Considering it was dark and the person was already disappearing from view, I'd say you're amazing to have caught that much."

"It leaves us with more questions, though," Greta said. "Does it make you nervous, Scarlett?"

"It makes me mad that someone was snooping around outside my house. Let's eat and get back to work."

"I can eat and work at the same time." Hal took one of the napkins Greta was handing out and wiped his mouth. "I've been analyzing our people of interest by how well they tell their stories and play their roles."

"An interesting approach," Luke said.

"Isn't it?" Hal said. "Sadly, they're all convincing. I wish I were auditioning them for a production of *Kidnapped*. I'd have an all-star cast."

"I picked up something from a true crime podcast," Winnie said. "If you want to understand a crime and catch the perpetrator, you need to understand the psychology of the victim. So, have we sufficiently examined what we learned from Quartz? From his stories?"

"What we learned from his movements too," Luke said.

"Henry was working on his movements today," Hal said. "I'll pick his brain tomorrow."

"I want visuals," Allie said. "I need to lay out the clues for a better picture."

"Anticipated." Scarlett took a stack of sticky notes and a marker from the mantelpiece and handed them to Allie. "I made a note for each clue in my notebook, and there are blanks for your personal brainstorms. The fireplace tiles make a great vision board. You can arrange and rearrange to your heart's content."

"You understand me so well." Allie snatched the tools and got to work.

"While Allie geeks out," Scarlett said, "I'll tell you about another person of interest, although he probably isn't the guy Luke saw disappearing tonight." She told them what she'd learned about Virgil.

"That's a sad wrinkle," Hal said. "Who or what is he supposed to have burgled?"

"The article didn't say. Nina's trying to find out more."

"Five days missing," Winnie said. "The police and coast guard are searching. Quartz might have gone with someone—such as the unknown waver from the video—Monday night and then might have fallen into a mine or a chasm, or he sank in a marsh, got stung by bees, or bitten by a snake." She sighed and spoke into her empty ice cream bowl. "Those are all possibilities, and the professionals have the investigation well in hand. With no results. And we haven't had results either. Sorry, but I can't help feeling gloomy."

"But we're accumulating suspects," Greta said. "Here, Winnie, take Cleo."

Winnie pulled Cleo onto her lap. "So many suspects, so little time."

"So many suspects for an unknown crime," Hal said. "Is it kidnapping? Abandonment? Murder? Your mood is catching, Winnie. Why don't you have enough cats to go around, Scarlett?"

"Sorry, Hal."

"Finished." Allie moved aside so the others could see the sticky notes.

"I'll need my telescope for the fine print from this distance," Hal said.

"It wouldn't help," Allie said. "It's a mess. I tried to put the clues in groups that made sense, but everything overlaps." She pointed to illustrate. "The Robert Louis Stevenson group is also part of the museum group and the Left Field Farm group. And when I tried to associate suspects with the groups, they overlapped too. Rylla and Tamsin go with all three groups." Allie sat back on her heels. "We're missing a clear front-runner for our suspect."

"We're also missing a motive," Luke said. "Why would any of these people kidnap or do away with Quartz? Or why cover up an accident?"

"Money," Scarlett said. "If they think he's got money or is coming into it."

"From recovering a lost manuscript," Greta said.

"I never knew a purring cat could be mood-enhancing," Winnie said, rubbing Cleo between the ears. "Here's another hypothesis. What if Adam is using his green thumb to help keep Left Field Farm afloat by trafficking rare orchids?"

"Maria did say that Sophie and the farm were in dire financial straits after her husband disappeared," Scarlett said.

"But would there be money in a scheme like that?" Allie asked. "Would Sophie go for it?"

"People go for all kinds of schemes," Hal said. "If she and Adam are into black-market orchids, then that's another reason Sophie wouldn't want people poking around the farm."

"Maybe she plays up stories about a mine to make sure people keep out, but the orchids are her real reason," Winnie said.

"So Quartz stumbled onto this operation and what?" Allie asked. "Do they have the place booby-trapped? I've seen that in movies."

"It happens in real life too," Luke said.

"How do we find out if it happened to Quartz?" Greta asked.

"Simple," Hal said. "We hand everything over to Nina and Andy."

"There hasn't been a ransom note. What does that tell us?" Allie asked.

"Are we sure about that? I mean, it's not as if the note would have come to us. Can we ask Nina if there's been one?" Scarlett asked.

"Call Chief Rodriguez rather than put Nina on the spot," Luke said. "Tell him about the suspected prowler too."

The others listened while Scarlett called Gabriel Rodriguez. She felt a lightening of spirits at his deep-voiced hello, though she detected a slight hesitation before he answered her question about a ransom note.

"As far as we've heard," he said, "no ransom has been demanded."

Scarlett looked at her friends as she asked the question they all dreaded. "Chief, does this mean there's no hope we'll find him alive?"

There was silence on the other end of the line for a long time. Finally, the chief said, "I don't know, Scarlett. I really don't."

16

Pastor Russ Coleman faced the Grace Church congregation as his wife, Martha, played the opening chords of the final hymn. "If you'll open your hymnals to page 218, we'll join the choir in singing 'Amazing Grace.'"

Scarlett opened her hymnal, and Luke put his hand on hers as they held the book between them. The beloved melody and words wrapped around her, giving her strength. "Amazing grace, how sweet the sound that saved a wretch like me."

She could sing it with her eyes shut, but kept them open, taking further strength from watching her friends in this peaceful setting. Luke beside her. Allie, Greta, and Hal in the pews ahead.

Chief Rodriguez in the choir. She loved that their chief of police had seriously considered following his heart into a career in opera. His booming baritone brought depth and resonance to the choir, though, and his clear-thinking logic led the police department on a steady path.

"I once was lost, but now am found. Was blind, but now I see."

After the service, as they joined the flow of congregants toward the doors, Luke murmured to her, "The chief just waved me down. He's parting the waters on his way to intercept us."

"Smiling or grim?" Scarlett asked.

"Like a man who wants to get home to his Sunday roast. Speaking of which, shall we ask Allie, Greta, and Hal to joins us for lunch at the Sandpiper?"

"Definitely." Scarlet turned at a tap on her shoulder.

"Peace be with you." Chief Rodriguez smiled, pressed a folded paper into her hand, and was out the door before she could return the greeting.

Scarlett unfolded the paper and read a note in the chief's block printing. *I find this line from Psalm 71 helpful: As for me, I will always have hope.*

"What is it?" Luke asked.

"A good man with a good message." Scarlett passed the note to him and went to invite the Barons and Allie to join them for lunch.

"Rain check?" Allie asked. "I have a date with the surf. I would have gone out this morning, but after last night church felt like the better place to be. My surfer buddies have had their eyes and ears out along the coast everywhere they've gone this week. No one's heard or seen anything."

Scarlett showed Allie the note from the chief.

Her friend's shoulders visibly relaxed. "Thank you, Scarlett. That helps. See you tomorrow."

Greta and Hal accepted the invitation. They walked down the street to the small eatery and ordered steaming bowls of soup and fresh rolls. The Sandpiper, though known as a bakery, dabbled in simple lunches.

Scarlett shared Chief Rodriguez's note when they sat down.

"We're off to clear our heads from all things hopeless this afternoon," Hal said.

"Where to?" Scarlett asked.

"The aquarium in Monterey. There's nothing quite like falling under the spell of jellyfish or watching sea otters play."

"Do you remember the bloom of brown sea nettles in the bay several years back?" Luke asked.

"Blooming nettles in the bay?" Scarlett asked.

"A massive swarm," Hal said. "Called brown, but they're bright orange, and they're jellyfish, not plants."

"There were literally millions of them," Luke said. "Bright orange, glowing, pulsating, and floating everywhere. One of the aquarium staff said it was like nature's lava lamp."

"Were they stinging anyone who got mixed up in them?" Scarlett wrapped her arms around herself.

"Come on, Ahab," Greta said to Hal. "Your talk of great glowing globs of jellies is not clearing thoughts of hopelessness or horror from anyone's head."

Scarlett forced a laugh, then she and Luke bid the Barons goodbye and went on to the farmers market.

Once there, Luke headed straight for a flower stall and bought an armful of sunflowers.

"Guaranteed to ward off brown stinging nettles and every other type of jellyfish," he said. "When you get home, put a vase of them in every room. If you see even one jellyfish within a block of your house, call and I'll get my money back."

"Deal," Scarlett said with a genuine laugh, then stopped abruptly. "Tamsin's here. Thank goodness."

"I'm glad to see her," Luke said. "But we're still suspicious of her, right?"

"Let's go talk to her and find out."

Farther along the row from the flower stall, Tamsin paid for several squashes. She put them in a string bag on her arm, then turned and saw Scarlett and Luke coming. "What a brilliant bunch of sunflowers. Well done."

"Nice to see you," Scarlett said. "How's it going? It's been a few days. Were you able to replace your laptop without too much hassle?"

"Aye, and my nose is firmly back at the grindstone."

"Are you finding much material locally for your project?" Luke asked.

The girl frowned. "Not heaps. It's rather like detective work and a treasure hunt rolled into one."

"What are you looking for?" Scarlett asked.

"Previously unknown primary sources by and about Stevenson," Tamsin said. "A tall order, but I've had a bit of luck in the Crescent Harbor Historical Society collections. Enough to keep me at it, anyway."

"That must please Maria," Scarlett said.

"It's early days," Tamsin said cryptically. She moved on to a stall selling a variety of peppers and tomatoes.

"I see fresh salsa in my future." Scarlett picked out jalapeños, poblanos, and red and yellow tomatoes.

Luke shifted the flowers in the crook of his arm and took the produce from Scarlett. "What's the most exciting thing you've found at the historical society?" he asked Tamsin.

"Several mentions of Jonathan Wright, the chap who owned the land where Left Field Farm is today. He was apparently a lighthouse keeper at one time."

"Farmer, miner, and lighthouse keeper. A man of interesting talents," Luke said.

Tamsin checked over the peppers, then settled on tomatoes and basil. "Stevenson's father was an engineer who built many of Scotland's lighthouses."

"That's a nice connection between the two men," Scarlett said. "Maybe they sat in the evenings talking about lighthouses."

"Stevenson had no love for them." Tamsin paid for the tomatoes and herbs before adding them to the string bag. "My dream is to find something Wright wrote while Stevenson convalesced with him. As a lighthouse keeper, he would have been used to keeping a daily log. It'd be grand if he continued the habit when that job was over. Kept a diary perhaps. Correspondence between the two men would be a gold mine."

"But no luck so far?" Luke asked.

"Not yet."

"It's good to have hope," Scarlett said.

"I prefer to help my hope along with action."

They reached the end of that row of stalls, and Scarlett saw the Left Field Farm stand around the corner. "Is that Adam Gray at Sophie's stall? Do you know him, Tamsin?"

"Vaguely, the way one does," Tamsin said. "I could use a bit of goat cheese. Nice bumping into you." She strode toward the stand.

"We've been dismissed," Scarlett told Luke. "How vague is 'vaguely, the way one does'?"

"I'd like to know how she helps her hope along with action," Luke said. "Oh, hey. Look who's watching the Left Field Farm stand."

"Henry. Is he watching the stand? It's hard to say. Will we blow his cover if we say hi?"

"I think we might, but here he comes. He's not bad at acting casual."

Henry meandered toward them as if he either hadn't seen them or didn't know them. When he bumped into Scarlett, he whispered, "Say nothing. I'm undercover." Aloud, he apologized, wandered over to a stand selling corn, then moseyed back toward the farm stand.

"The market is full of intrigue today," Luke said.

"I'm certainly intrigued," Scarlett said. "Have you met Adam? I haven't. He's big. Almost intimidating."

"Wait," Luke said. "You, who thumb your nose at two rattlesnakes at a time, find the man in the red flannel shirt intimidating?"

"Absolutely. His muscles have muscles. And is Tamsin flirting with him? We don't know much about him, do we?"

"We could go stock up on goat cheese. Make small talk."

"Let's leave him to Henry," Scarlett said. "I'd rather follow Greta and Hal's lead and clear my head this afternoon. Perhaps with a load of laundry. Nah, with quiet time with a cat and a book. How about you?"

"I have an idea for getting to know Adam better. It needs fleshing out, though." Luke's phone buzzed with a text. "Here's my call to duty."

Scarlett's heart sank. "Are you leaving?"

"No, it's a reminder to get a report in tonight. Ready?" He offered his arm to Scarlett. She took it and glanced back at Adam.

What don't we know about you, Gray Ghost?

⁂

Scarlett's phone rang just as she'd decided to be a grown-up and start a load of laundry. "Saved by the ring tone and an unknown caller, Cleo. Hello?"

"This is Virgil Soto, Ms. McCormick. Do you know that quartz crystal supposedly helps with retaining what you learn?"

"I didn't."

"It'd be handy if it worked, but I'm not so sure it does," Virgil said. "Quartz Sutton shared that little nugget with me, and it's taken me this long to remember what I told you I'd forgotten."

"Oh?"

"It wasn't something I wanted to tell Quartz. It's something that belongs to him. He asked me to hold on to it for him. Would you be willing to come see it for yourself and tell me what to do with it?"

"What is it?"

"I don't know. He passed it over to me in an old stationery box, and I haven't opened it. A book maybe."

"I'd love to see it, Virgil," Scarlett said. No matter how innocent the little old man seemed, she was not going over there alone. "May I bring a friend?"

"I love company," Virgil said.

"Thank you. We'll see you soon." Scarlett hung up and considered her options. Luke would be working on his report, so she called Winnie.

"Is it Quartz's mysterious package?" Winnie asked.

"Fingers crossed."

"Pick me up in five."

Ten minutes later, a beaming Virgil opened his door at their knock. Scarlett introduced Winnie.

"Nice to meet you," he said.

"The pleasure is mine."

"Come on in," Virgil said. "I set our friend's box on a chair in the parlor. You've been here before, Scarlett. You and I will go first so we can get the full effect of how Winnie reacts to my gizmos, gadgets, and thingamajigs."

Winnie's reaction to the shelves of contraptions was everything Virgil must have wanted. She rotated in a circle with her serious eyes as bright as the shining brass. "May I please come play at your house someday, Virgil?"

"A playdate, like my great-grandsons." Virgil chuckled and nodded to one of the chairs. "There it is. Go on and open it."

Scarlett picked up the faded blue box that had once held notepaper and envelopes. She and Winnie sat, Scarlett with the box on her lap. Virgil sat across from them.

"First," Scarlett said and handed the box to Winnie. "Does it weigh about right for the mysterious package?"

Winnie nodded and handed it back.

"Then here goes." Scarlett lifted the lid. Inside, a leather-bound book was nestled in tissue paper. The name *Jonathan Wright*, embossed in gilt, gleamed on the cover. Scarlett took the book from the box and leafed through several pages that were covered in small, precise script.

"Jonathan Wright's diary," she breathed. She gaped at Virgil. "Quartz didn't show you? He didn't tell you what this is?"

"If he had, I might've remembered it sooner."

"Do you know where Quartz got it?" Winnie asked.

"Don't know a thing about it but that he thought it was something special."

"It is." Scarlett continued leafing through the pages and came across entries made in September 1879. "Winnie, listen. 'My daughters badgered Mr. Stevenson to write a story for them. He would not, he told them. They must write one with him. They have, and now they've hidden it. Like pirate's treasure, they say.' Oh, and read this." The neat, legible handwriting gave way to a poorly spelled childish scrawl on the next page.

Cluse to ore treshur
Done go in winder
Kip yor feed dry
Sos yu done cry
An yu chant bee sore
When yu reed ore store

Scarlett laughed. "If these are clues, they make about as much sense as anything we got from Quartz."

"Should we take a picture of that page?" Winnie asked.

"It's tempting, but no," Scarlett said. "I'd rather believe that Quartz will be back. Then he can take charge of the treasure hunt."

"I remembered his box last night," Virgil said. "Late. Or maybe early. Dark, anyway. Someone tried to get in."

"Did you call the police?" Winnie asked.

"Wasn't any need. My alarm scared him off."

"We should call them now and let them take the diary for safekeeping," Scarlett said. "If I'm right, they kept it for Quartz once before." She called Nina, told her about the diary and burglary attempt, then assured her that she and Winnie would stay with Virgil until she arrived.

"We all grew fond of Quartz in a very short time," Winnie said. "So thanks for getting in touch with us."

"I'd like to see the old coot again, myself."

"We're doing our best to make that happen," Scarlett said. While they waited, she read them random entries from the diary.

When someone rapped on the front door, Virgil went to answer and came back with Nina.

She greeted Scarlett and Winnie, then took the chair Virgil offered. "Scarlett said you think someone tried to get in last night, Mr. Soto."

"I know so."

"And you scared them off?"

"My alarm did."

"I wish more people were smart and had alarms," Nina said. "Did you see the person or a vehicle that might be involved?"

"No."

"Do you know why Mr. Sutton asked you to keep the diary for him?"

"No."

"You didn't ask him why?"

"I've never made a habit of asking nosy questions," Virgil said.

Nina smiled. "And I often wish I didn't have to. Did Mr. Sutton seem worried or preoccupied when he asked you to keep the diary?"

"If I were nosier, maybe I would've noticed. I'm sorry. I wish I had."

"But you took good care of his package," Nina said. "When we find him, I know he'll be grateful. In the meantime, we'll have extra patrols drive past your house."

"That'll be nice. Like having more company."

"I'm afraid they won't be stopping in," Nina said.

"Understood."

"Have you had a lot of company lately?" Scarlett asked.

"Not so much, but more than usual. Quartz, you and your friends, and that young woman with the Scottish accent."

17

"Kudos for recovering the mysterious package," Allie said when Scarlett arrived at the museum Monday morning. "I whooped out loud when I got your text."

"I heard you all the way to my house. Cleo yowled along with you."

"A cat with excellent taste." Allie handed Scarlett her morning coffee. "Not that I ever doubt you, but are we sure it's the mysterious package?"

"Until we hear otherwise from Quartz himself, I'll believe it is."

"Two questions, then," Allie said. "First, was Virgil's prowler after the diary to grab the treasure for him or herself? And second, what was Tamsin doing there?"

Scarlett looked at Allie over the rim of her cup. "Those are the million-doubloon questions." She took her coffee up to her office, reading back through the texts from Greta, Hal, and Luke the night before. They'd bubbled over with excitement about the diary too, with the good news begetting good spirits. Even diving back into her Black Death research didn't cast a pall on the morning.

A text arrived from Greta midway through the morning. *Can you spare a few minutes? Henry is here. Would like to give progress report.*

Does he know about the diary? Scarlett sent back.

That's your story to tell.

Meet in my office?

Hal, Henry, and Winnie on the way, Greta sent. *I have a tour in a few. Will catch up later.*

Scarlett heard Hal and Henry approaching her door as Hal told Henry he didn't have to keep apologizing. At the door, the men stood aside for Winnie to enter first. Winnie rolled her eyes subtly at Scarlett when Henry apologized again.

"Hi, guys," Scarlett said. "Sit down and let's hear this progress report."

"Good morning, Scarlett." Henry slumped into a chair. "Hal says I shouldn't, but I must apologize for taking advantage of my welcome at the Reed."

Hal's eye roll wasn't at all subtle, but if Henry noticed, he didn't show it.

"You're fine, Henry," Scarlett said.

"I think of the museum as the hub of the investigation."

"Very astute, Henry," Hal said. "It is the hub."

Henry sat up straighter. "My report, then. I've determined there's a connection between Quartz, Tamsin Murchie, and the lost Stevenson manuscripts. I'm just not sure what the connection is."

"Can you share the steps that led to your determination?" Winnie asked. "It's not that I'm questioning your research," she added when he sagged in his chair. "I'm in the security business and take every opportunity to hone my skills. I liked the idea of your clean-slate method. I'm sure I can learn something from you."

"I'm sure my methods are embarrassingly primitive compared to yours." Henry's hands twisted around each other. "My work is by no means conclusive. I'm at a point where I'd like to know if what I have matches where your investigation has been heading."

"The connection between Quartz, Tamsin, and the manuscripts is one of the directions we've been heading," Scarlett said. "We've been hunting for a common thread that runs through the mishmash of information we've collected. That connection seems to be a pretty sturdy one."

"Especially since a certain phone call yesterday afternoon," Hal said. "Tell him, Scarlett." But before she could speak, he blurted, "She found Quartz's package."

Henry's mouth dropped open.

"I simply answered a phone call," Scarlett said. She told him about the call from Virgil, the diary, the prowler, and Tamsin's visit.

"Fantastic," Henry said. "Did you take pictures of the treasure hunt clues?"

Tickled at his growing excitement, Scarlett wished she had. She explained her reasons for refraining and was glad when Henry agreed.

"This news ties in with what I overheard between Tamsin and Adam at the farmers market," Henry said. "How did you like my undercover act?"

"You were superb. Henry 'bumped' into Luke and me, at the market yesterday," Scarlett told Winnie and Hal. "So he could stealthily let us know we shouldn't give him away while he surveilled the Left Field Farm stall."

"I couldn't make sense of what Tamsin and Adam were talking about," Henry said. "Now the pieces are falling into place. She talked about a diary and said she was terribly keen to get her hands on it."

"Wow," Winnie said.

Hal nodded. "And how."

"I wonder if Tamsin and Adam are in cahoots," Henry said.

"That could explain the friction between Tamsin and Rylla," Scarlett said. "And the friction between Rylla and Adam."

"It could," Winnie said. "Here's something I've been wrestling with. We don't know what the story is behind Virgil's arrest for burglary. How do we know Quartz gave him the diary willingly? What if he took it?"

"Then why did he call me yesterday and hand it over?" Scarlett asked.

"If he took pictures of the pages with the information he needed,"

Winnie said, "or that someone else needed, then he could maintain his innocence because he appears compliant at this point."

"I wish you hadn't thought of that," Scarlett said. "But as Luke would probably say, stranger things have happened. Have you met Virgil, Henry?"

"Haven't met him, no, but Hal told me who he is. We planned to stop in on our whirlwind tour of places Quartz visited, but we spent too much time in Danielle's rabbit hole of a shop."

"You loved it," Hal said. "Admit it."

"Guilty. You could lose far more than an afternoon in there. You could lose a whole a group of social historians for a week. She really has a fantastic eye."

"But you didn't buy a thing," Hal said.

"So I'll go back sometime. For now, I need to focus." Henry leaned toward Hal. "Your pal Virgil is a crook. Didn't it occur to you that he could be in cahoots with Tamsin?"

"All of this seems so unlikely," Scarlett said.

"Don't be fooled." Henry turned to her. "Tell me about him. You've been in his house. What's it like?"

"I haven't seen much of anything outside the parlor," Scarlett said. "He loves antique brass contraptions. The parlor is like a museum for clockwork mechanisms."

"I don't see how they fit into the picture," Henry said.

"That's been our problem all along," Scarlett said. "Pieces that don't fit. We haven't gotten very far at trying to put them together into a clear picture. But for what it's worth, I do think you're wrong about Virgil. The burglary charge never went anywhere and it was ten years ago."

"And you've met the man and taken your own measure of him. That counts for something," Henry conceded. "Can we agree that barring accident or kidnapping—for which there's no evidence—the diary and the search for a lost manuscript are at the center of the mystery?"

Although she, Winnie, and Hal nodded in agreement, Scarlett didn't feel the bubbly lift of spirits she'd felt the night before when they'd exchanged texts.

"Thank you for listening and indulging me." Henry stood to go. "You're kind to let me take so much of your time."

"You're always welcome," Scarlett said.

Hal also left, intent on catching up with Greta after her tour. Winnie stayed.

"What do you think?" Scarlett asked her.

"That we still have no evidence of anything much."

"But we have the diary," Scarlett said. "Well, the police have it."

"So what I think," Winnie said, "is that you should give this theory about the connection between Quartz, the diary, a manuscript, and Tamsin to the police too."

"That sounds like a good idea, especially since a walk to the station might clear my head. I'll call to see if Nina or Andy is in."

⁂

Nina leaned her elbows on her desk. Andy Riggle sat in the other guest chair next to Scarlett. Both officers listened intently as she laid out the theory.

"Interesting," Andy said when she'd finished.

"Thanks, as always, for bringing that to us," Nina said. "There are a few things we can tell you. First, Adam's and Virgil's cases are simply old news."

Scarlett felt a measure of relief. "Good."

"We can also tell you that we can't place Tamsin at the beach the night Quartz disappeared," Andy said.

"You asked her about her whereabouts?"

"Yes, for that night and also Saturday night, when someone prowled your house and tried to get in Virgil's."

Nina picked up where Andy left off. "She was home alone. So there's no one to corroborate, but there's no evidence to prove otherwise either."

"We also found no evidence of a burglary at her apartment," Andy said, "other than the missing laptop and her word that it is missing. But that, in itself, doesn't mean she lied."

The conversation volleyed back to Nina. "It might actually prove that she's telling the truth. That someone wanted the laptop and took it quickly and cleanly."

"Someone is out there prowling around at night," Andy said. "I checked around your house. We believe you that there was someone, but again, there's no evidence."

"And still no trace of Quartz," Scarlett said.

"We're putting together a team," Nina said. "They're going to check the abandoned mine on Sophie Morata's farm."

On the walk back to the museum, Scarlett took out her field notebook. She opened it, and a folded paper fluttered to the ground. She picked the paper up and smiled at the note from Chief Rodriguez. She would always have hope, but they also needed evidence.

She texted Greta, Hal, Winnie, and Allie. *Meeting in my office, 2:00.*

Allie closed the coffee shop at two on weekdays. She was the last to arrive in Scarlett's office. "Winnie told us about the Tamsin theory. You should know I came to your meeting instead of surfing."

"I love you too, Allie." Scarlett took a deep breath. "We've got work to do. We need evidence."

"To strengthen the case against Tamsin?" Greta asked.

"Yes. Nina and Andy haven't found anything that clearly implicates her, but no evidence doesn't mean no crime. Let's try going at this from multiple directions. We'll search for evidence to support the Tamsin theory. At the same time, we'll try to clear our other suspects from suspicion."

"Who are we clearing?" Hal asked.

"Rylla, Sophie, and Adam." Scarlett shrugged. "We might end up clearing Tamsin."

"But that gets us somewhere," Greta said. "I want to dig even deeper into Tamsin's background."

Winnie nodded. "She has hidden depths."

"Rylla's in the gallery," Allie said.

"Why don't you and I go talk to her?" Scarlett suggested. "And, Winnie, after that, let's go talk to Virgil again."

"What's my assignment?" Hal asked.

"You and Henry work well together," Scarlett said. "Why don't you show him all our notes? Go over them for anything we've missed. He'll have fresh eyes."

"I'll search for Sophie online," Winnie said. "What about Adam?"

"Luke's working on something," Scarlett said. "Everyone ready? Let's go do it."

Rylla raised her head from her sketching when Scarlett and Allie approached. "I don't mean to sound rude, but why do I deserve so much of your attention?"

"Simple," Allie said. "We want to find Quartz."

Rylla raised an eyebrow at Scarlett. "What's your guess for today?"

"Rainbow finch."

"Nope. As for Quartz, I've told you everything I know."

"We're actually trying to clear people from suspicion," Allie said. "Can you help us do that with anything you can tell us about Sophie?"

"I don't know Sophie from Adam. Small joke."

"You've never talked to her?" Scarlett asked.

"All I know about Sophie is that she doesn't want to be known." Rylla erased some shading. "Sophie might not even know herself. She's like my favorite bird—destined to be forever unknown by you."

"One more question," Scarlett said. "Does Adam raise orchids?"

Rylla gave a weary headshake. "Isn't there a museum around here somewhere you should be running?"

Allie and Scarlett managed to wait until they'd left the gallery before bursting into laughter. They stopped laughing when they saw a distraught Hal and a despondent Henry in the lobby.

"I made the mistake of telling him the police have no evidence against Tamsin," Hal said.

Henry sat hunched on one of the lobby benches. "I've never felt less certain of seeing Quartz again." He stared at the floor. "I should be out there searching for him. But where? And how? I'm not fit like I used to be. I'd end up in trouble myself. A hindrance. A nuisance."

"We can search," Hal insisted. "That's what I've been trying to tell you. I have all our notes on my phone. We'll go over them together. You'll bring fresh eyes to them. 'But screw your courage to the sticking place and we'll not fail.'"

Henry looked up. "Macbeth?"

"Never say that word," Hal said. "Please. The Scottish play."

"You theater people. Historians can't afford to be superstitious."

"Virgil, do you mind a terribly nosy question?" Scarlett asked.

Virgil, obviously delighted at another visit, had invited them into the parlor again. "I don't ask them myself, but go ahead."

"Why were you arrested for burglary ten years ago?"

To her surprise, Virgil cackled until his eyes watered. "Unintended consequences. I was demonstrating my antique burglar alarm. Thought I'd hooked an investor so I could make and sell them. Come on to the front door, and I'll show you."

They went with him, and he picked up a gadget from the floor. Shaped like a doorstop, it was made of brass with scrollwork along its sides.

"From the 1870s. Knob on this side, see? You wind it." He wound it, then lifted an inch-long lever set into the incline of the wedge, so that the lever stood upright. "Now, I'll step outside, then you slip the thin edge of the wedge under the door so the lever sticks upright against the door."

"Like a doorstop?" Winnie asked.

"Best doorstop in the world. See what happens when I try to get back in."

Virgil went out and Winnie positioned the wedge.

"Ready?" Virgil called.

"Ready."

Virgil pushed the door. The door pushed the lever. The lever activated an amazingly loud bell inside the wedge.

Grinning, Winnie pulled the wedge away and let Virgil in. "I love this thing. Did you ever make them to sell?"

"Not after that mess with the investor. I'm happier puttering."

"What happened?" Winnie asked.

"I did that demonstration for him at his house and the dirty dog called the police on me. Claimed I broke in to steal his metalworking tools."

"That's terrible," Scarlett said.

"They couldn't make the charges stick of course." Virgil cackled again. "I got myself a slick lawyer. My granddaughter. So good she graduated law school early."

On the way back to the museum, Scarlett's and Winnie's phones both buzzed with texts.

"From Greta," Winnie said.

"Read it."

"She says, 'Pay dirt. Tamsin has been in our area before. A few years back, she worked with a group of historical archaeologists excavating in caves. In the comments section of an article, Tamsin answered a question about a cave in Big Sur. She described it as difficult to get in and out of, and hard to find. Said she wouldn't disclose its location, joking that it's the perfect place to hide out, as long as there's enough food and water. Or, if needed, to hide a body.'"

18

"When shall we five meet again?" Hal intoned. "In thunder, lightning, or in rain?"

"There'll be six of us," Scarlett said. "Luke will want to be in on it. Seven if Henry comes too."

Scarlett and Winnie had returned to the museum and Scarlett's office. Allie, Greta, and Hal met them there.

"He's gone back to the motel," Hal said. "I sent him our notes so he can read them on his laptop. I think my feelings are hurt. After I pulled him out of his wallow of depression, he said he works better alone."

"I think you're happy he's not constantly telling you what to think," Greta said.

Hal grinned. "How well you know me."

"So what's the next step?" Allie asked. "We need a plan. We need a plan for making a plan."

"Which comes first, the plan or the place to hatch it?" Greta asked. "We need someplace safe. At this point I don't feel like that's our house or Scarlett's. They've both been prowled."

"We could come back here," Scarlett said. "An after-hours museum meeting. That's not really ideal, though."

"It would also be unusual," Winnie said. "We don't know who's keeping tabs, but let's not draw attention to ourselves or the museum. May I suggest we meet at my place? It's a loft, so no one can listen at the windows."

Scarlett gave Cleo an extra treat after supper that night, glad that the cat didn't glare up at her with suspicion. "Thank you, Cleo. I appreciate your acceptance of this bribe. I don't know how late I'll be tonight, and I might come home with a feather or two on me from Mac."

Cleo was always intrigued by the occasional feather that came home on a pant leg or a sleeve. She cleaned her face and paws, then lifted her nose to sniff the air.

"No more now, my friend. But if we're lucky this evening and make our plans well, we might retrieve Quartz. Then you'll have a chance to meet him and make a new friend with your charming ways."

The doorbell rang.

Scarlett looked at the time. "Luke's fifteen minutes early. Hold down the fort until I'm back, Cleo." Scarlett grabbed her purse and coat, checked to be sure Cleo wasn't poised to make a break for freedom, and opened the door.

No one was there.

Scarlett felt a chill wind, then realized the wind wasn't there either. It was her own fear sliding like ice down her spine.

She slammed the door, locked it, and double-checked the lock. She double-checked the locks on the back door and all the windows too. She slipped into her coat, to calm the shiver she suddenly couldn't control, and perched on the edge of a kitchen chair. She felt like a meerkat on alert.

When the doorbell rang again, she called Luke, without moving from the chair. "Is that you at the door?"

"Yes. Why?"

"Tell you in a sec." She shook herself and went to check the peephole. Luke stood outside, studying a piece of paper the size of a postcard. Scarlett opened the door with her best approximation of an everything's-normal smile. "Hi. What are you reading?" She stepped out and closed the door behind her.

Luke's automatic "hi" didn't sound any more normal than Scarlett's, and he wore what she thought of as his FBI face. He reached around her and tried the door. She'd locked it, so it didn't open.

"The paper?" she asked. "What is it?"

"Show you in the car," he said with a quick smile. She didn't mind when he put his arm around her. The way he surveyed the street in both directions as they headed for his car started the shivers again.

"My doorbell rang about fifteen minutes ago," she admitted.

"Yeah?" He stared toward the end of the block as he opened the car door for her. "Who was it?"

"No one."

"Did you see anyone anywhere?"

"I didn't spend much time looking. As soon as I realized no one was there, I shut the door and locked it."

He closed her door and went around to his. When he got in, the locks engaged with a click. The sleek black sedan felt as secure as Fort Knox. She watched him take a plastic bag from the glove compartment and slip the paper inside.

"What is that?" she asked.

"A note I found on your doormat. It's a scare tactic, Scarlett. Pure. and simple. Don't read anything into it. Don't let it rattle you."

"You mean more than you've rattled me just now by saying all that?"

"Good point. Sorry. Do you want to see it?"

"Yes."

"Hold the bag by the edges." Luke handed it to her.

The note was a cliché straight from an old movie with a message spelled out with letters cut from newspapers and magazines. Scarlett read it aloud. "'Let the dead bury the dead.' Lovely. Is it okay to take a picture of it?"

"Sure."

"Let's drop it off at the police station before we go to Winnie's."

"I probably haven't told you often enough that you're an amazingly strong woman." Luke started the car. It purred as smoothly as Cleo, but he waited for her to take the picture before putting it in gear.

"If this note is about Quartz, I don't care if someone wants me to believe he's dead," Scarlett said. "I will always have hope. Also, I'm going to invite Nina and Andy along to Winnie's with us."

They drove the short distance to the police station in silence. Scarlett set the note in its bag on the console between them. She didn't want to touch it any more than was absolutely necessary.

"Isn't that Nina?" Luke nodded toward a woman coming out the front door. "Want to catch her?"

Scarlett grabbed the bag with the note and hopped out of the car.

Nina saw her and came to meet her. "I thought you'd be at Winnie's by now. I'm on my way over." A pleased grin lit her face at what must have been a very surprised expression from Scarlett. "It's not often I can shock you so thoroughly, Scarlett. Hal invited me to the meeting."

"Perfect. I was going to invite you and Andy after I showed you the present someone left on my doormat."

"Uh-oh."

They waited for Luke to park, then went inside together. Scarlett put the bag on Nina's desk. As she told Nina how it had been delivered, Scarlett saw Chief Rodriguez leaning in the doorway, listening.

"I'm sorry this happened to you," Nina said. "We'll check it for fingerprints. Luke is probably right that it's meant to scare you more than anything else. And I probably don't need to tell you, but be sure you keep your doors and windows locked." She sat back with hands splayed on the desk. "The sooner we figure this out and tie it up, the better. Let's go see what we can do about that tonight."

※

Winnie lived in the converted loft of a building sandwiched between the Greek to Me Playhouse and Glass Act, a glassblowing art studio. The buildings were located in what used to be Crescent Harbor's small industrial district. The industrial vibe of the neighborhood suited Winnie, matching her aesthetic of no-nonsense simplicity. Her loft suited her even more—practicality with a dash of unexpected elegance. Mac, Winnie's parrot who had free reign of the loft, added a touch of whimsy.

"You're stuck with me representing the police force," Nina told the assembled friends when they'd all found a place to sit. "Andy has a rare night off."

"Your civilian clothes say that you were planning a night off too," Allie said.

"Going for a lower profile," Nina said. "To keep the prowler guessing."

"Mac is on duty," Winnie said. "He'll let us know if anyone comes up the stairs to listen at the door."

"Good," Greta said. "Between Mac and the height of your windows, your loft offers distinct advantages for this meeting."

"Another advantage is the abundance of samosas in my kitchen," Winnie said. "My mother made more than I can eat in a month, or even two. Help yourselves." She passed around a warm platter of the crispy triangular pastries containing a mixture of spiced potato and peas.

"Delicious," Greta said. "Thank you. Now let's get started. Hal has put together a solid plan."

"Greta and I went to the aquarium yesterday to clear our heads," Hal said. "It made all the difference."

"Was it the day away, the aquarium, or the jellyfish and otters that made the difference?" Scarlett asked. "It's a serious question. I'm a true believer in head clearing."

"Some of each. But when I put this plan together, the aquarium displays I enjoy most swam back into my mind." Hal gave a quick smile. "They're displays of communities. Schools of fish swimming in formation. Otters playing together, holding hands as they float on their backs." He reached over and took Greta's hand.

"That's what all of us here do," Greta said. "We work together and stick together."

"Now," Hal said, "because someone separated Quartz from his community, my plan calls for a communal effort to get him back."

"Nina, are you here because the police are willing to help with the plan?" Scarlett asked.

"Chief Rodriguez is aware of this meeting and the basic outline of the plan," Nina said. "When we're through here, I'll fill him in so he can sign off on it officially. If he'd known about the samosas, of course, he would be here right now."

"Are you seeing him in person after the meeting or calling him?" Winnie asked.

"I'll meet him back at the station."

"Then I'll send some back with you."

"Deal," Nina said. "There's something else we should talk about before the plan." She told them about the anonymous note left on Scarlett's doormat.

"That's hideous," Allie said. "Is it a threat? A warning?"

"It's the words of a coward and a bully," Luke said, and his voice echoed in the loft. "Sorry. Didn't mean to say that so loud."

"The rest of you might receive similar messages too," Nina said. "If you do, call us. We're taking this as seriously as every other incident associated with Quartz's disappearance."

"Why are we sure he's still alive?" Allie asked quietly.

Scarlett looked at the others. None of them offered an immediate answer, but she had one that had become her litany. "Hope," she said, thumping her fist on the chair arm. "And I meant to say that so loudly."

"Scarlett's right," Hal said. "On to the plan?"

They nodded, and Hal moved from beside Greta to sit on one of the tall stools from Winnie's dining area.

"All our suspects have proven themselves to be good actors," Hal said. "Now they're going to help us put on a play." He swept his arm to encompass all of them. "We are the main cast. Rylla, Sophie, Adam, and Henry are the extras. Tamsin is the audience."

Winnie raised her hand. "Why is Henry an extra?"

"He's likely to become emotional when he hears we're on the verge of rescuing Quartz," Greta said.

"It'll be a completely natural and believable reaction," Hal said. "That's what will make him nail his performance, which will push Tamsin to act."

"Are we following a script?" Allie asked.

"A loose script," Hal said. "For us, it starts tonight, when Nina and Chief Rodriguez give the okay. Then we'll call the extras and ask them to meet us at the museum before it opens tomorrow morning. Make it eight thirty. We'll tell them we want their help to catch the person who lured Quartz into the mine at Left Field Farm and trapped him there." Hal smiled at Nina. "Nina has the leading role tomorrow morning."

"I'm not sure I'm up for that," Nina said.

"Your script is short and easy to remember," Hal said. "If you forget a line, I'll feed it to you by asking a question. I'll send you the script when I get home. Main cast, please arrive by eight."

"Why would this work?" Allie asked.

"It might not," Hal admitted. "But the script will set up a scenario that should make Tamsin think if she doesn't get to Quartz quickly, then all her work will be for nothing." He chopped a hand through the air. "Cut. Forget should, would, could. I'm going with *will*. The extras, by their reactions, will convince Tamsin she needs to act. That action—leading us to Quartz—will be her confession."

"Is it right to play on Henry's emotions like this?" Winnie asked.

"I've been torn," Hal said. "Greta knows him better and made a good point."

"We're planning a rescue." Greta's voice was soft. "But to be realistic, it might be a recovery. The trek to the cave will be hard enough. If Henry comes with us and falls apart when we get there, then we'll be dealing with how to get him out of there too."

Nina gave a curt nod. "I'll have a first aid kit with me."

"So then, tonight's assignments," Hal said. "Winnie will call Rylla, Greta will call Henry, and Scarlett will call Tamsin. We won't refer to this as a play or tell them who else will be at the meeting. If they ask questions, we'll tell them to save them to ask in the morning. Nina, you'll call Sophie with a different message. Tell her Adam and Luke are going into her abandoned mine to rescue Quartz, with police and others standing by. Luke, you've been talking to Adam?"

"He's ready."

"Good. Everyone here, except Luke, will be at tomorrow's meeting. Luke will be at the farm. If all goes well, two cars will follow Tamsin. Nina and Scarlett in one, Greta and me in the other. Allie and Winnie, you'll be at the museum because someone needs to be there." Hal crossed his fingers. "And in case of a glitch."

"It's a lot of moving parts," Winnie said. "Lots of opportunities for unintended problems."

"To quote a Scottish poet," Hal said, "'The best laid plans of mice and men gang aft agley.'"

"Is that Stevenson?" Allie asked.

Scarlett shook her head. "Robert Burns."

Luke groaned. "Burns? I'd rather that fire didn't enter into this in any shape or form."

"Sorry to be a bucket of cold water when we're all fired up," Winnie said, "but what if Tamsin doesn't lead you to Quartz?"

"I think she will," Scarlett said. "Sunday, at the farmers market, she told Luke and me that she likes to help her hope along with action. At the time, we weren't sure what that meant."

"It sounds pragmatic," Winnie said.

Allie nodded her agreement. "Also ruthless."

"You're both right," Scarlett said. "So what do you get when you add ruthlessness, pragmatism, and a desire for action? Pure villainy."

19

Scarlett disconnected from her call to Tamsin. She pressed herself into the corner of the sofa, troubled by Tamsin's reaction—cool, matter-of-fact, unsurprised.

"Tomorrow morning? I should be able to manage that," Tamsin had said without even the slightest hint of tension or surprise in her voice. "If there's nothing else, good night."

How could a message asking for help at the scene of the rescue of a man, imprisoned for days at the bottom of a mineshaft, not come as a surprise? *But maybe I'm projecting. Everything about this situation has been surprising to me. But to a villain?* She'd used that word earlier at Winnie's. It didn't sit right with her. But again, nothing about the situation sat right.

Cleo hopped into Scarlett's lap, vying for room with her laptop.

Scarlett adjusted her crossed legs, the cat, and the computer, and pulled up the photograph of the anonymous note. *Let the dead bury the dead.* With its snipped letters, glued in slanted and wavering lines, the note was almost laughable. Being laughable almost helped make it feel less personal. Almost.

The uppercase *L* was familiar. Decorative. *And why does it make me hungry?* Scarlett glanced at Cleo, and realization dawned. *Fish tacos, that's why.* She didn't say it out loud in case Cleo thought she was offering another treat. She'd spoiled her enough since she'd come home and checked the door and window locks again. Scarlett navigated to The Salty Dog's website, clicked on the menu, and scrolled through it.

"There, Cleo. Our anonymous bully snipped the *L* from their 'Landlubber's Linguini.' Score one for knowing menus because of eating out too often. That tells us—well. It doesn't tell us anything we don't already know." She clicked back to the note. She'd tell Nina in the morning, but it probably wasn't anything more than a piece of anonymous note trivia. "Except the note isn't anonymous. Tamsin is responsible. She's responsible for all of it. And to think I liked her."

She stroked Cleo. "Thank you for bringing my blood pressure down, Cleo. Maybe I'll be able to look at Tamsin tomorrow morning without bopping her." She yawned, then jumped when her phone buzzed with a text. *Sounds like a rattlesnake*, she thought.

The text was from Luke. *Everything okay?*

All quiet here. Do you think anyone else found a note on their doorstep when they got home?

If we're lucky, yes.

Scarlett, eyes wide, sent back a series of question marks.

It would mean you're not the only one in this nut's crosshairs.

You mean in Tamsin's crosshairs.

That's what I said, Luke wrote. *Tamsin, nut—what's the difference? Makes me sad. And mad.*

From ghosties and ghoulies and long-legged nutters, may the good Lord deliver us. A lullaby from Scottish wisdom and me to you. Sleep well, Scarlett.

I'll try, Scarlett sent. *You too.*

⁂

Morning came sooner than Scarlett would have liked, yet hadn't come fast enough. She sent a quick text to Luke. *Sleep report. Wouldn't say I slept well, but no nightmares.*

Always a plus. Take good care today, he wrote back.

You too. Rescuing Quartz would be a definite plus.

Scarlett searched for Cleo. Not on top of or under the covers. She found her on the floor at the foot of the bed, giving herself a luxurious bath in a square of morning sunlight.

"Lovely as ever, Cleo. So what do you, with your exquisite taste, recommend wearing to a rescue party in a cave?"

Cleo was too busy with her ablutions to answer.

Scarlett grabbed her robe. "Never mind. I'll figure it out over breakfast."

Cleo beat her to the kitchen. Scarlett measured kibble into the cat's automatic feeder and felt her own stomach flutter as she thought of the day ahead. She made herself sit and eat a bowl of oatmeal with a handful of almonds and walnuts, knowing she'd need the solid breakfast for stamina to get her through the day. She tried to relax her mind by channeling a former colleague in New York. Anytime that particular friend felt down or overwhelmed, she counteracted it by dressing to the nines and taking extra care with her makeup.

"That won't cut it for me today, Cleo. For one thing, dressing to the nines won't mesh well with my activities for the day. But more importantly, I'm not down or overwhelmed."

Cleo paraded past with her tail held high.

"You're right. I was tempted to say that I'm scared to death. But I'm not scared, either. I'm determined." She stood up. "I'm strong. I'll be surrounded by strong, determined friends."

Hal's play called for them to act as though they were heading for the farm and a hike to the mine. Jeans, T-shirt under a flannel shirt, and hiking boots worked for that—or for a trek through the wilderness to find a cave and a man who may or may not be alive.

As Scarlett dressed, Cleo circled her ankles, rubbing against them. "You are a sterling example of calm, Cleo. Except in the presence of catnip or fresh fish." Scarlett glanced at the faint trail of black fuzz on her jeans. "But I'll accept your gift of fluff and emulate your calm today by being one with the fur."

She grabbed a fleece and a hoodie, then found an old blanket and dug a backpack from the closet. A small first aid kit, bottles of water, granola bars, and a flashlight went in the pack. She would carry the pack on the hike. The blanket and extra layers would be in Nina's vehicle in case they were needed afterward.

Scarlett scanned her peaceful living room to make sure everything was in order, then she opened the curtains and gave Cleo a firm kiss between the ears. Time for the curtain to rise on their play.

"Coffee," Allie said as she, Scarlett, and Winnie entered the museum a few minutes before eight. "That's shorthand for good morning, and all I can say until I drink some."

"Bad night?" Scarlett asked.

"I might have slept better if I hadn't been worrying about how you'd sleep after that anonymous note."

"Same here," Winnie said. "I can't even come up with a suitable pun. I'm worried about Rylla too. She'll be here."

"How did she react when you called her?" Scarlett asked.

"I thought she might cry."

"Not Tamsin," Scarlett said. "She was disturbingly collected. Icy enough to make me shiver."

"Caves are cold," Winnie said. "Do you think she gave Quartz a blanket?"

"I have to believe she did," Scarlett said. "Food and water too. Otherwise why take him alive?"

She and Winnie watched Allie work her coffee machine magic.

"Do you know what Emily Dickinson said about hope?" Winnie asked. "It's the thing with feathers." She pulled one of Mac's feathers from a pocket of her jeans. "For good luck."

Greta and Hal arrived looking serious.

"We found a note when we got home," Greta told them. "Slipped under the windshield wiper on Quartz's truck."

"How awful," Allie said. "The same message that Scarlett got or something worse?"

"The same," Hal said. "Henry had one too. We dropped ours at the police station on the way here."

"I took a picture of mine and couldn't help staring at it last night," Scarlett said. "The *L* in the note is from The Salty Dog's menu."

Winnie shook her head. "This whole thing is so bizarre."

"But we have a good plan, thanks to Hal," Scarlett said, "and we'll make it work."

Hal drew in a deep breath, shook out his arms, and gazed at each of them in turn. "It begins."

"Nina's not here." Scarlett heard the edge in her voice. "Shouldn't we wait?" *And should we worry?* Glancing at Allie and Winnie, she could tell they were thinking along the same lines.

"She'll be here," Greta said.

"Nina's going to be great," Hal said. "She even suggested a small rewrite to her part of the script to ratchet up the drama. We're seeing an example of it right now."

"Well, ratchet it back down a tad, will you?" Allie said. "By now I'm not sure I should have a cup of coffee."

"She's going to arrive after our extras are here," Hal said. "Give them a chance to shuffle their feet and wonder what's going on, much as you are, and give Tamsin time to sweat a little more."

"Nice touch," Scarlett said.

"But now that we know that, will we be able to act our parts convincingly?" Winnie asked.

"Without a doubt," Hal said. "Nerves are contagious."

By 8:38, the contagion was obvious. Nina still hadn't arrived. Neither had Rylla. Tamsin and Henry looked toward the door, toward each other, shifted their feet. Quiet conversations started and stopped. Allie had made repeated trips from standing next to Scarlett to her coffee counter, checking the morning's brew, cream, napkin dispensers, stirrers, and everything else she'd already checked. Greta and Hal remained silent, with strained faces, standing hand in hand. Winnie drummed her fingers on the door, watching the parking lot. Scarlett's nerves jittered along with everyone else's.

"Refill, Henry?" Allie asked on her next circuit between the coffee shop and the lobby.

"Thanks, yes."

"Tamsin? Have you changed your mind? I can do tea."

"No. Thanks."

Scarlett noted the pause between Tamsin's "no" and her "thanks." *Guilty nerves*, she thought. *Worried about her own skin. She doesn't know Rylla should be here, so she's certainly not worried about her.* Scarlett's heart skipped a beat. What if Rylla hadn't arrived because something had happened to her? Panic rose in her throat. *Stop that*, she told herself firmly. *Panic won't help anyone.*

She checked her phone. No texts or phone messages. She glanced at Hal. With his eyebrows and mouth drawn, he watched the door. *Is he acting, or—?* But then she saw him relax and heard Winnie unlocking the door.

"Sorry I'm late," Rylla said as she passed Winnie. "At least I made it before Officer Garcia."

Marching in on Rylla's heels, Nina arrived in a uniform that appeared triple starched for the occasion. Boots, belt, and badge gleamed with recent polish. Her hat gave her extra height and impressive presence. Scarlett and the others instinctively drew closer together and faced Nina.

"Thank you for waiting for me." Nina stood at parade rest with her hands clasped behind her. "I'm here this morning to let you know that there are crucial developments in Mr. Sutton's case. We now possess an antique diary, belonging to Mr. Sutton, that he left with an acquaintance for safekeeping. Mr. Sutton told his acquaintance that the diary gives the coded location of a lost Robert Louis Stevenson manuscript. According to his acquaintance, Mr. Sutton keeps the key to the code in a secret pocket sewn into his jacket."

Excited exclamations broke out until Nina shushed them.

"We're convinced Mr. Sutton is trapped in the abandoned mine on Sophie Morata's land. We've put together a team of experienced spelunkers. They'll descend the mineshaft this morning to rescue him."

"I have a bad feeling about this," Rylla said.

"Police and EMTs will be there to assist," Nina told Rylla. "We'll do our best to get him out as safely as possible, but we'd like Quartz's friends, old and new, to be there. He'll need your good wishes and encouragement after his ordeal."

"And, with luck, we'll witness the recovery of a lost Stevenson manuscript," Tamsin said. "May I document the rescue and recovery with my camera?"

"You're welcome to bring your camera," Nina said, "but permission for filming will have to come from Chief Rodriguez, Ms. Morata, and ultimately Mr. Sutton."

"If you don't mind, then, I'll see everyone at Left Field Farm after I collect my camera from my flat."

"What is it with guys and dangerous ideas of fun and heroics?" Rylla closed her eyes, her skin as pale as if she'd seen a dozen rattlesnakes. "I'm heading out there now."

"I can't imagine what came over the old fool to do that on his own," Henry said. "The lust for treasure, I guess." He shook his head. "I need directions to the farm," he said to Nina. "Greta, Hal, I'll see you out there."

With Tamsin and Rylla already gone, Winnie locked the door behind Henry.

"Now Act Two begins," Hal said. "And was I right or was I right? No one needed a single acting lesson. Everyone looked convincingly worried and upset."

"Because we *are* worried and upset," Greta said, "and we need to hurry if we don't want to lose Tamsin and end Act Two early."

They dashed from the museum with good luck wishes from Allie and Winnie. Scarlett hopped into Nina's unmarked police SUV. They headed for Tamsin's apartment with Hal and Greta close behind. They pulled over, with a clear view of Tamsin's dark-blue Nissan compact, and waited. And waited.

"We missed her," Scarlett said.

"No. Andy stayed in the museum parking lot during our meeting and followed her so we wouldn't lose her. Sit tight."

Ten minutes later, Tamsin left her apartment with a backpack slung over one shoulder and climbed into the compact, then drove away. They followed at a careful distance.

"Where's Andy now?" Scarlett asked.

"Behind Hal and Greta. Relax."

That was when Act Two swerved off the rails.

"She missed a turn," Scarlett said, agitation mounting. "This isn't the road to Big Sur. She isn't taking us to the cave."

Nina radioed ahead to Chief Rodriguez at the farm. "We're behind the suspect. Suspect is travelling toward Left Field Farm."

"Rylla Summerville is already here," Chief Rodriguez said.

"Henry Lang?" Nina asked.

"Negative."

"He might have stopped somewhere first," Nina said.

"No." Scarlett felt sick with the realization. "He's the one we should have followed."

20

"It's Henry?" Nina asked. "Scarlett, are you sure?"

"Fairly sure. We need to find him."

"Not good enough." Nina hit a button on the radio. "Chief, we'll be in touch." She hit another button. "Andy, we're pulling her over. Follow my lead." To Scarlett, she said, "Hold on tight."

Nina put on her lights and siren, rocketing past the vehicles they'd let get between the police SUV and the Nissan. Another burst of the siren encouraged Tamsin to pull off the road at a small shopping center and park. Nina pulled behind her at an angle, so she had Tamsin in view and effectively blocked from reversing. Andy parked on the passenger side of the Nissan. Hal and Greta pulled in beside the SUV.

Tamsin remained in her car. Scarlett imagined her either frozen or quaking with fear.

The two officers conferred, then approached Tamsin's car.

Scarlett lowered her window to listen in. Hal and Greta lowered theirs as well.

"What's going on?" Hal stage-whispered to Scarlett.

"Plot twist."

"Always welcome," Hal said.

"Maybe not this time. We've made a mistake. Henry has Quartz, not Tamsin."

The Barons gaped at her. "We wondered why we weren't on the road to Big Sur," Hal murmured.

They heard Nina ask Tamsin to unlock her door, then show her hands and keep them where she could see them. Tamsin obeyed. Nina opened the door and asked Tamsin to step out.

"I don't understand." Tamsin's voice shook. Her eyes, huge and glistening with tears, didn't leave Nina's face.

"Do you know where Quartz Sutton is?" Nina asked.

"You told us he's in the mine. Tha-that's where I'm going," Tamsin stuttered. "You told us to. You said I could fetch my camera." She shook her head slowly back and forth. "I don't understand."

"We followed you from the museum." Andy came around the front of the Nissan. "We expected you to lead us to a cave in Big Sur where you worked an excavation several years ago."

"Whatever for?" Tears ran down Tamsin's cheeks.

Hal, watching Tamsin intently, said, "She's not acting."

"That was my impression as well." Scarlett got out and scooted between the SUV and Nissan. "Nina, Andy, sorry, but this is doing us no good, and it's not going to help Quartz either. What we need to do is find Henry."

"Scarlett, get back in—" Nina started to say.

Tamsin cut in. "He knows the cave."

"Henry does?" Scarlett asked.

"He was along on the same dig," Tamsin said. "That cave is a perfect place to hide someone away."

"You knew Henry Lang before you came to Crescent Harbor?" Andy asked.

"I did."

"So the two of you are working together," Andy said.

"What?" The color drained from Tamsin's face. "No, never."

"Nina, please," Scarlett said.

"Right," Nina said. "Henry's way ahead of us. Tamsin, can you lead us to that cave?"

"Aye. Anything to help."

"Then you'll ride with us. Up front." Nina grinned at Scarlett. "Scarlett, hop in back. Tamsin gets VIP treatment."

Tamsin grabbed the backpack from her car and locked it.

Andy stopped her before she got in the SUV. He asked her to open the pack and show him the contents.

"VIP treatment with conditions," Nina corrected herself.

Greta leaned across Hal and called through the window. "Scarlett, do you mean it? Henry?"

"Greta, I'm so sorry."

"You have nothing to be sorry about," Greta said as her expression hardened. "That scoundrel has a lot to answer for when we catch up with him."

"Scarlett," Hal said, "call us when we're underway and entertain us with your expert reasoning for this jolt to our beautifully constructed play."

When Andy was satisfied that there was nothing dangerous in the bag, he opened the SUV's door for Tamsin. Then he called to Hal. "Any problems driving ten to twenty over the limit?"

"It'll be my pleasure," Hal said.

"I'm sure it will. You keep up with Officer Garcia. I'll be right behind you."

Scarlett and Nina slid into the SUV. "Welcome aboard," Nina said to Tamsin as she put the vehicle in drive. "We'll take the road around Crescent Harbor and pick up the coast highway on the other side. Buckle up."

They headed back the way they'd come at top speed. Hesitantly, Scarlett chanced interrupting Nina's concentration with a question. "Nina, do you mind if I call Greta and Hal and tell them how I know it's Henry?"

"Please do. Andy and I are sticking our necks out on this. Not that I don't trust you, Scarlett, but—"

"But we still don't have any evidence," Scarlett finished for her.

"That's it." Nina maneuvered the SUV into the left lane, the siren and lights shooing cars coming toward them onto the shoulder.

"For what it's worth, coming from a former suspect, I don't believe you are sticking your neck out, Officer Garcia," Tamsin said.

Scarlett admired the spunk in her voice. Then, as they swung back into the right lane, she saw Tamsin's knuckles whiten as she grabbed the handle over her window.

Tamsin drew in a breath. "That said, I'd like to hear Scarlett's reasoning, as well."

Scarlett called Greta on speakerphone.

Greta answered without so much as a hello. "I'm furious with him."

"Save your anger for the hike," Scarlett said. "It'll improve your energy reserves. Put me on speaker so Hal can hear while I apologize for hitting on this realization too late to do us the most good."

"Forget the self-recriminations," Hal said. "Spill."

"We've said all along it's about the stories," Scarlett said. "This started with Henry's stories from the very beginning. Think back. They're full of discrepancies. Starting with when Quartz planned to arrive and how long he planned to stay. That information, or lack thereof, came from Henry. Quartz was under the impression you expected him Friday. He also seemed to think you expected him to be around for days and days."

"The man who came to stay," Greta said.

"Henry told you the motels were full. That's why he begged the favor of a room at your house. But he had no trouble finding a motel room when he showed up. He didn't use the word 'diary' before we did, but—actually, hang on, Greta." Scarlett leaned forward. "Tamsin, at the farmers market on Sunday, did you tell Adam how great it would be to find Jonathan Wright's diary?"

Tamsin blinked in surprise. "No. We talked about how great goat cheese is with walnuts on pasta."

"He's such a fraud, Greta," Scarlett said.

"A manipulative piece of work," Greta agreed.

"And of course he got an anonymous note. He made them himself. And that business about not being in shape to go out searching for Quartz. How many times must he have hiked to the cave?"

"The cave," Tamsin said with a shiver. "May I tell you why I believe Professor Lang did do this?"

"Please do." Scarlett handed the phone to Tamsin. "Start with why you pretended you didn't know him when we met in the lobby this morning."

"I didn't let on that I know him, because I do know him too well," Tamsin said. "What he's really like. There were a few problems on the excavation. The sort of problems that make you wonder how an instructor is allowed to stay on."

"Oh dear," Scarlett said.

"I saw him at the farmers market and prayed he didn't remember me from the dig. He wasn't in charge—just along for the experience, I guess. I managed to avoid him well enough. I actually don't think he remembers me at all."

"Because his eye is only on what he wants," Nina said.

"A couple of the other graduate students threatened to lodge complaints with his college," Tamsin said. "He left weeks before we were finished." She gave Scarlett's phone back.

"I can't believe this. How could I have been so wrong about him?" Greta asked.

"He played his part well," Hal assured her. "When things like this happen, the one to blame is the one who lied, not the one who trusted him."

"I'm going to stop distracting the drivers with this conversation.

We'll see you at the cave." Scarlett hung up and texted Winnie. *Tamsin cleared. Details later. Will you research Henry's background, with attention to student complaints against him?*

They sped along a narrow, winding highway that clung to steep coastal cliffs, giving spectacular views of the Pacific. If Scarlett concentrated on the views, she could almost forget how close they were to the edge and how very far below them that water sparkled in the sun.

"We want the road near the state park," Tamsin said, almost to herself. "We should be getting close."

Nina relayed the information to Andy. Not knowing how close they were to Henry, they switched off the lights and sirens. Tamsin pointed out a sign for the road. They steered onto a narrower road, following its rutted surface until they came to a more primitive single-lane. Tamsin directed Nina to take it, and they climbed into the mountains.

"We'd be better off on mules," Nina muttered as they thumped into yet another pothole.

"There are two wider places ahead," Tamsin said. "We always parked in the first and turned around in the second."

Even at a crawl, the SUV bounced and scraped. After several steep switchbacks, they came to the first widened area to find a red Mini Cooper already parked there. Nina parked beside it, and Hal and Andy pulled in alongside them. While Nina ran a check on the first car's license plate, Scarlett and the others got out and stretched.

"That's Henry's," Nina said as she joined them. "Tamsin, can you find the cave from here?"

"Aye. It's a fair hike up to the cave. About an hour."

"Everyone think they can make it?" Nina asked. "We don't know what we'll find when we get there either, so there's no need to say yes."

"I think we're all in this," Greta said.

The others nodded.

"All right," Andy said. "We're entering an area that's currently closed to the public. The chief arranged permissions. Let's not do anything to make him sorry about that."

"And let me tell you what to do if we see a mountain lion," Nina said. "It isn't likely, but it's better to be prepared."

"Better to be prepared than to be a snack." Andy hitched a backpack over his shoulders.

"If you see one," Nina said, "make yourself as big as you can. Open your jacket. Raise your arms. Attacks are incredibly rare, as they tend to avoid humans. But if you're attacked, fight with everything you have."

"Tamsin, did you see any mountain lions when you were here excavating the cave?" Hal asked.

"No. We did see condors. Huge things. Much larger than turkey vultures. You can hear their wing beats for half a mile. The trail's this way."

When they reached the trail, Nina went first, followed by Tamsin. Andy brought up the rear. The trail took them down along a creek, kicking up dust as they passed prickly pear and an impressive amount of poison oak. They followed the creek and then started uphill, scrambling at times as the path rose and grew narrower.

Nina slowed her stride. "Not recommended for the faint of heart."

"And that is never us," Hal said. "For we are here to snare he who is false of heart."

"False of heart. I like that," Nina said.

Scarlett gently shushed them. "We don't know how far ahead he is, so shouldn't we be stealthier?"

"Truth is truth," Hal said. "Verily, I shall zip it."

The dirt path rose through a stand of live oaks, then to a field of boulders.

"Tamsin?" Nina said. "What now?"

"There's a landmark. A long, horizontal boulder."

The others peered at her.

"I promise. It isn't the sort of thing one forgets. We climb over the boulder and the trail picks up on the other side. We're very nearly there. Another ten minutes."

Tamsin took the lead and her memory proved accurate. They picked up the path, and skirted a bluff. Nina and Andy took the lead with Tamsin right behind. When she tapped Nina's arm, they all stopped. Andy put his hand to his ear. They heard indistinct voices.

"The cave," Tamsin whispered. She pointed ahead and to their left, about fifteen feet away.

"I know that voice," Greta whispered. "Henry."

Another noise—a hissing, snorting sound—froze them.

Scarlett used the same hushed tone. "Mountain lion?"

"Oh my word." Nina pointed above them at two massive birds in a tree. "They're as big as Buicks."

"Condors," Tamsin said softly.

The condors weren't at all happy to see them. They hissed again, snorted, and took to the air. The sound of their great wings felt like a drumbeat. Their soaring flight mesmerized the group.

And maybe Henry too. She crept forward and saw him at the cave opening, watching the condors glide and turn.

As the magnificent birds wheeled back toward the cave's bluff, Henry gave a yelp and ducked out of sight. She heard him snarl, "If you didn't hide the code in your jacket, then where is it, you old fool?"

Scarlett edged closer to the entrance and peeked in. Quartz was slumped against the cave wall, his ankles chained. Henry loomed over him. When the other man didn't answer quickly enough for Henry's liking, he slapped Quartz.

"Hey!" Scarlett shouted without thinking.

Henry whirled, then sneered and ran toward her. "You're next."

21

Scarlett braced herself. When Henry tried to tackle her, she shoved him with all her might. To her shock, he sprawled onto the hard floor of the cave—and didn't move.

The reality of her actions hit. *What was I thinking? What have I done to Henry?* She knelt beside him. He lay on his back, eyes closed. She touched his hand. "Henry?"

Henry's eyes popped open, then went wide as he stared past her, shrieking, "She's trying to kill me! Get her off!" He punched at Scarlett, then rolled away in a protective ball, letting out a tremendous moan.

"This cave is a crime scene," Andy announced as the others entered the cave. "Ms. Murchie, Mr. and Mrs. Baron, you'll have to stay outside."

What have I done? Scarlett felt like rolling into a ball too.

"Hey, you all right?" A kind hand landed on Scarlett's shoulder, and Nina crouched down beside her.

"I wasn't trying to kill him. He slapped Quartz. I—"

"I'll sue you for every penny you have," Henry snarled.

"He's lying," Quartz said in a surprisingly strong voice. "Officers, I witnessed the entire thing. Henry went for Scarlett. She resisted, and he tripped. What you see is the end of the story."

"She attacked me," Henry howled. "Slammed my head into the ground. Punched me when I was down."

Overwhelmed by what she'd done, unable to speak, Scarlett nodded at Nina.

Nina leaned in close to Scarlett's ear and said, "Quartz is a sterling witness. Do not say another word."

"Your head didn't actually slam into the ground, and I can see the rock you tripped over at your feet," Andy said. "Mr. Sutton, is this where you've been sleeping?"

"If you can call it sleep." Quartz got to his feet and rattled the chain.

Scarlett realized she was kneeling on a sleeping bag.

Andy lifted the end of the bag and exposed a thick layer of pine branches. "Mr. Lang, did you cut these branches and pile them here, or did you bring them with you?"

"I cut them. I'm an expert woodsman."

"All the comforts and amenities of home," Hal called from the mouth of the cave. "If you don't mind being in chains."

"Thank you, Mr. Baron, but we have this under control," Nina told him. "This won't take long. Scarlett, can you stand? Walk?"

"I think I'm all right."

"I want you to be sure. It's a long walk back."

Scarlett stood and put her weight on one foot, then the other. "I'm fine."

"Then please stand with the others outside the cave."

"How about me?" Quartz asked. "I'd like to stand out there in the fresh air too."

"Mr. Lang," Nina said.

"What?"

"The key to Mr. Sutton's chains. Now."

Andy got the key from Henry. He tossed it to Nina, and she unlocked the leg irons.

"Thank you," Quartz said with a quiver in his voice. "I would hug you or kiss you or both, but I smell like something that even a condor wouldn't go near."

As Quartz joined his rescuers outside the cave, Andy snapped handcuffs on Henry's wrists. "Henry Lang, I'm placing you under arrest for the kidnapping of Quinn Sutton, also known as Quartz Sutton, and for holding him against his will."

Henry blustered. At a glare from Andy, he subsided.

Andy continued, "I'm also arresting you for making an unpermitted and unlawful camp on public lands and for illegal timber harvest." Andy read Henry his rights and asked if he understood them.

"Of course I understand them," Henry answered with a sneer.

The officer ignored the tone. "Are you able to stand, Mr. Lang? Will you be able to hike out of here?"

"I'm certainly capable if she is." Henry nodded at Scarlett. "But I don't want that woman anywhere near me."

"That's fine, Mr. Lang," Nina said. "Because you'll be my hiking partner." She took his elbow. "Hal, can you give Quartz a hand if he needs it?"

"We'll all take turns with that," Greta said. She grinned at Quartz. "Even if he does smell."

"Right then," Nina said. "Officer Riggle will stay to process the crime scene. Let's move out."

Andy had his backpack off and open.

Scarlett laid a hand on his shoulder. "Thanks, Andy."

"Hey, thank you." He sat back on his heels. "And I'm sorry we let you down."

"How on earth do you think you let me down?"

"The condors came swooping back to the tree and I'm not ashamed to admit we all quietly freaked out about them. By the time we realized you'd gone on ahead, the show in the cave was over. Except for the show Mr. Lang put on when he saw Nina and me. You could have been seriously injured, and that would have been all our fault."

"I don't want to hear anything against those beautiful birds," Scarlett said with a chuckle. "They distracted Henry too. That's how I got close enough to surprise him. See you later, Andy."

She trotted along the path until she caught up with Tamsin at the rear of the rescue group.

"There you are," Tamsin said. "We took bets as to whether you'd flown off on a condor or were riding a mountain lion bareback straight down the side of the mountain. Quartz came up with those options."

"Have you asked him about Wright's diary and the lost manuscript?"

"Do you know, I thought that would be the first thing I'd ask him about. But no. It's his story to tell, and I'll be happy to hear it, but not until he's ready."

Up ahead, Scarlett heard Quartz telling Hal and Greta how he'd entertained himself during his hours in captivity. "I spent part of every morning and afternoon doing calisthenics and what I called limited-range hikes. Three steps to the right, three steps back to center, three steps left. More regular exercise than I've had in years."

"But how did that happen?" Greta asked. "How did he get you to go with him and how did he get you chained up?"

Quartz shook his head. "Maybe later, Greta. The memory of that is still raw."

"Fair enough," Hal said.

"But did you see what he did with the chain?" Quartz said. "He fixed a large eyebolt up high into the cave wall. When he did that I don't know."

"Sounds like premeditation," Scarlett said.

"Doesn't it?" Quartz said. "Such an excellent brain he has. My goodness." He shook his head. "Henry told me he'd seen eyebolts like that screwed into rock faces closer to the coast, supposedly used for tying up great masted sailing ships in days of yore."

"A bit of history with your misery." Greta frowned and then flatly said, "Lovely."

"If he'd set the eyebolt lower down, I would have tried chipping it out of the wall with my belt buckle," Quartz said.

"Ingenious," Hal said.

"Thank you. I imagine I'd still be chipping away at it ten years from now. I did try to yank the chain from the wall. Good arm exercise but ultimately fruitless as a means of escape."

Nina called a halt halfway back for a rest and water. Henry accepted a bottle of water from Nina without a word. He sat on a rock and raised the bottle to his lips with his cuffed hands. If he'd said anything along the way, Scarlett hadn't heard. She shared her granola bars and water bottles with Tamsin and Quartz. Greta and Hal had their own.

Quartz eased down onto another rock and sipped slowly. "Ah, warm water never tasted so good. You have to admit, Henry, you weren't overly generous with water or food." He set the bottle on the ground and opened the granola bar.

"Thirst and hunger are an incentive," Henry said. "That's why I didn't put you up at a five-star hotel either." As he got up, he casually kicked over Quartz's bottle.

No one said anything, but they all glared at him. It turned out to be more effective than gasps or shouts, as Henry shrank from them and moved closer to Nina.

The group remained quiet the rest of the way down. When they reached the cars, Nina put Henry in the back of her SUV.

"May I say something to him before we go?" Quartz asked.

Nina studied his face, then nodded. "I guess you've earned it." She lowered Henry's window several inches.

"Henry, I wanted to tell you how sorry I am," Quartz said.

Henry glared. "What are you talking about?"

"For whatever happened in your past that made you this way, so that you thought you had to lie and steal and hurt to get what you wanted. I was your friend, Henry. I wish you'd been mine."

Henry spluttered until Nina raised the window.

"I meant every word of that," Quartz said. "I hate to lose a friend."

Nina peered at Quartz's face. "I need you to stop by the hospital. Have your condition checked and documented. Hal, Greta, will you take him?"

"Of course."

"Tamsin, I'd like you to ride back with them."

Tamsin nodded. "Happy to. Officer Garcia, if you remember the emails deleted from my laptop and cloud storage, may I suggest you look for them on Mr. Lang's electronic devices? Try the Sent folder."

"It'll be my pleasure," Nina said. "Scarlett, you're with me. We'll need to get your statement at the station."

"Sure." Scarlett's stomach twisted with worry. Despite Nina's and Andy's reassurances, she wasn't sure how Chief Rodriguez would view her rash act. *And then there's Henry threatening a lawsuit.* She gulped.

Nina directed Hal in a series of incremental, nail-biting maneuvers to get their car turned around on the narrow road. She waved them on their way, then repeated the procedure with the SUV. Scarlett didn't close her eyes, but wished she could close her ears to Henry's terrified whining.

"Calm down," Nina told him when she had them bumping back toward the highway. "How many times did you have to do that yourself?"

"I drive a Mini Cooper, not a monster. What's going to happen to it? You can't just leave it back there."

"Worried a condor might fly off with it?" Nina whooped, startling Scarlett and making Henry cringe. "They were amazing. Do you know how lucky we were to see them? Absolutely primitive and gorgeous."

"Bird of a lifetime," Scarlett said. "Rylla will be as green as her hair with envy."

Henry frowned. "Arrested by a maniac. I can't believe this is happening."

"You didn't have much to say on the hike out," Nina said.

"I was saving my breath. I offered that old fool money. More money than he's ever seen."

"Mr. Lang," Nina said, "you said you understood your rights. I suggest you not say more until your lawyer is present."

"More money than any of you have seen. And then you attacked me," he snapped at Scarlett.

Nina repeated the Miranda rights and then asked Henry if he understood.

"I already said I did."

"I'm going to start recording our conversation. Do you understand?"

He scowled. "Yes."

"Ms. McCormick, you're a witness to this recording, but I'd like you to refrain from speaking. Do you understand?"

"Yes."

Henry went on with his rant. "I could've sold the manuscript and been out of the country by now if the old fool's truck weren't such a wreck."

"Are you talking about Mr. Sutton?" Nina asked.

"Of course."

"Did you kidnap him?"

"That was his fault. He had a choice. He could've sold the diary to me. He refused. So I had to get it another way. After getting him into the cave, if I'd been able to get rid of his truck, everyone would've thought he'd left town. I would've had plenty of time to make him tell me where the diary was."

"How did you know about the diary?" Nina asked.

"He told me about it. What did he expect me to do? Sit by and watch him find a treasure like an undiscovered Stevenson manuscript? And when I asked if he had a buyer lined up for the manuscript, he said he wasn't interested in making money off it. Unbelievable. I found a buyer in no time. All it took was a few emails."

"Why that cave?" Nina asked.

"Because it's perfect, and so was my plan. I took part in an excavation there several years ago. We all joked about it being the perfect place to hide a body. How did you find it?"

"We're good at our jobs," Nina said. "Did you meet up with Quartz on the beach Monday night?"

"The fool actually believed it was a coincidence. I'd been following him, waiting for the chance to lure him to the cave."

Nina didn't "How did you?"

"Easy. I asked if he wanted to see a safe quicksilver mine. It was even easier when we got to the cave."

"Slipped him a sedative?" Nina asked.

"Enough to get the leg irons on and make him understand how he could earn the right to have them off again. His fault he didn't listen. His rust bucket of a truck didn't help. It was stuck in front of precious Greta's house, so everyone was crying, 'Oh, woe, Quartz is missing.'"

"Did you break into Tamsin Murchie's apartment and take her laptop?"

Henry lifted his chin a notch. "Of course. So many of my genius touches helped make her look guilty."

"Did you break into Mr. Sutton's truck?"

"I didn't have to break in. I had his keys. Anyway, it was hardly worth it."

"Were you snooping around Left Field Farm Tuesday?"

"Not snooping. Taking a nice walk in the woods."

Nina hesitated but didn't respond to the ridiculous comment. "Did you try to break into Virgil Soto's house Saturday night?"

"If it hadn't been for his alarm, that diary and the manuscript would be mine. He's an even bigger fool than Quartz."

"Did you snoop outside Scarlett's house Saturday night?"

Henry snickered. "And scared her cat."

"Did you leave anonymous notes at the Barons' and Scarlett's?"

He narrowed his eyes. "You won't be able to prove it."

"Don't bet on it," Nina said.

"Do you know what makes me happy?" Henry asked.

Neither Nina nor Scarlett answered.

"You should learn to be more curious," he said. "I'll tell you anyway. It's that nonsense that Quartz has the coded message and the key."

"We know he doesn't have it," Nina said. "The message is in the diary."

"And he doesn't have the first clue what the message means. It's all been for nothing. He doesn't win anything," Henry crowed. "Nothing at all."

"Officer Garcia," Scarlett said, "may I ask him one question?"

"Go ahead."

Scarlett met Henry's gaze. "Were you going to let him go?"

"Don't pretend you're a fool. You know I couldn't."

She'd once thought Henry was as intimidating as a teddy bear. Now his words and the deadly cold in his eyes chilled her soul.

22

Hours later, Scarlett still couldn't shake the memory of Henry's eyes. Cleo met her with purrs and a loving headbutt when she walked through her front door late that afternoon. Scarlett scooped her up and took refuge in the cat's slow blinking eyes. "Your eyes have the wisdom of ages, Cleo. Cat ages, anyway. It is so good to be home and away from all of that. And now I'm starving. Let's go scrounge."

As soon as Scarlett set her down, Cleo led the way with her tail up. Scarlett dropped her backpack on a kitchen chair. While she found bread, lettuce, and mayo in the fridge, Cleo took in the variety of interesting smells that had come home on her jeans and boots. Scarlett took tuna from the cupboard and sent Cleo into raptures of fish-longing when she ran the can opener around the rim.

She gave Cleo a couple of spoonfuls, then made herself a thick sandwich. She didn't bother to sit before taking a bite. "Oh, yum." The sandwich really hit the spot. She took her plate to the table, intending to check messages on her phone, but finished the sandwich first. She hopped back up and dished out a big bowl of ice cream.

"Saving lives is hungry business," she told Cleo. "All that adrenaline. And fear." She shivered and ate the rest of her ice cream slowly. As she wiped her mouth, a text came in from Winnie.

Results from your research request, Winnie sent. *Hints and allegations in Henry's background from years ago, but nothing in the last two years.*

That seemed to back up Tamsin's story. *Send that info to Nina and Andy*, Scarlett sent.

Quartz rescued? Winnie asked.

We got him. He's safe. Details in group text later. A group text would save her having to repeat herself.

Scarlett did the dishes, willing a text from Luke to interrupt her. She hadn't heard from him and, when she'd asked, Nina had only said she didn't have any information to share. She couldn't tell if that was a kind, official way of sidestepping the question. She didn't press it. Nina had given her a generous amount of leeway on their expedition.

Dishes done, Scarlett propped herself up in the corner of the sofa and sent a text to Greta to ask how Quartz was doing. While she waited for an answer, she composed the group text. In light detail, she told them about the plot twist and happy outcome. She relayed seeing condors close up, but not about shoving Henry. She didn't tell them about Henry's unnerving eyes either. Before she hit *Send*, Greta's answer arrived.

The hospital says he's in good shape. Slight dehydration. Hungry, which they say is a good sign. They'll keep him overnight for observation.

So good to hear, Scarlett wrote back. *Will include that in group text about basic details of our trip.*

Greta replied with a thumbs-up.

Scarlett added Greta's information to her text and sent it to Luke, Allie, Winnie, Greta, and Hal. Cleo joined her on the sofa, curling up on her lap. "Who's as brave as a mountain lion and black as a California condor? You are, Queen Cleopatra."

Allie sent a smiley face and three thumbs-up. Winnie wrote that she and Mac wished they'd seen condors.

Between the exertions and emotions of the day and the rumbling purr of a good cat, Scarlett was drifting off when Luke called.

"Hey there," he said. "I just got home and read your text. How do you feel?"

"I hate to say it, but I was nodding off when you called."

"Can you wake up enough to grab a bite?"

"I was starving when I got home, so I've already pigged out on a sandwich and ice cream."

"I don't blame you." He laughed.

She laughed too, then sobered. "How did it go at the mine?"

"Billy Engler's remains have been recovered. Sophie took it hard."

"Oh no."

"Don't worry. She's in good hands. Rylla took over like a mother hen."

"Sophie let her?" Scarlett asked.

"Rylla is an odd little bird, but it was incredibly sweet. Speaking of birds, tell me about the condors."

They talked until Scarlett yawned. He congratulated her again on a rescue mission well done and wished her sweet dreams.

Greta and Hal invited the group of actors and extras to a celebration dinner several nights later. Sophie, Rylla, Adam, and Andy sent their regrets. "It's still a good crowd," Hal said as he handed Scarlett and Luke glasses of wine. "A fine audience for Quartz. Check it out." Hal nodded toward the living room.

"I used to be a bit of a rebel," Quartz said. He sat in an overstuffed chair, one leg crossed over the other, hands clasped comfortably on his stomach. "But after that experience, I'll admit I definitely feel more like rubble."

His audience—Allie, Winnie, Nina, and Tamsin—laughed.

"Henry made a mistake," Quartz continued. "If he'd wanted to break me, he shouldn't have left the measly amount of food and water that he did. I was determined to survive, if only to have one more decent meal in my life."

"He made a few more mistakes than that." Greta paused to hug Quartz around the shoulders before going back to passing around a plate of samosas that Winnie had brought.

"His name is appropriate, though," Tamsin said. "He turned out to have a Jekyll-and-Hyde personality, and Dr. Jekyll's first name was Henry."

"And our friend Stevenson wrote that excellent story," Quartz said.

"Your mysterious package," Winnie said. "Why did you mail it to yourself?"

"A safety precaution that I wouldn't have needed if not for my own big mouth. I told people I'd found a primary source that gave the location of a lost Stevenson manuscript. I didn't go into detail, except to say the location was hidden in a coded message." Quartz shrugged. "Several people besides Henry wanted to get their hands on the manuscript and knew I held the key. When I realized someone was sniffing around my place, watching me, I mailed the diary to myself, care of the museum. I thought I could outwit the snoop. I didn't realize it was my friend Henry."

"It's no wonder my vision board was a mess," Allie said. "We didn't suspect Henry at all."

"He was already in Crescent Harbor when he called Greta to ask if you could stay," Nina said. "He booked a motel room under a false name, paid in cash, and set his plan in motion. The district attorney says Henry will be going away for a long time."

"He blamed your truck for ruining that plan," Scarlett told Quartz.

"My valuable, rusty, loyal, decrepit truck? What did that innocent vehicle ever do to him?"

"It wouldn't start, so he couldn't move it and make people believe you'd gone off somewhere on your own."

Quartz adopted a superior tone. "Starting it takes skill."

"He blamed a lot things for 'making' him come up with the plan and for bringing it down," Nina said. "Thrillers, TV shows, and movies. Because in his words, they 'make it seem too easy.'"

"As a historian, shouldn't he have stuck to primary sources?" Luke asked.

Greta sniffed. "Any true historian would."

Hal called everyone to dinner. They helped themselves to the dishes set out in the dining room and took their plates back to the living room.

Quartz ate sparingly, but complimented the food profusely.

"Are you all right?" Scarlett asked him quietly.

"Fine, fine. It'll just take a few days for the old appetite to catch up with the rest of me." He set his plate on an end table. "I'm sorry I didn't have time to lay out all my clues so that you could figure out what my mysterious package was all about. I was still working them out myself when Henry grabbed me."

"You talked about stories and mentioned your own diary," Hal said.

"Yes. Good."

"That first night, at the opening, you spent the most time with the Wyeth paintings," Luke said. "The illustrations from *Treasure Island*."

"Were you avoiding Tamsin?" Scarlett asked Quartz.

"Ah." Quartz sheepishly apologized to Tamsin. "The little time I spent with you, I could see you were sharp, so I did stay away. I was afraid you might be after the diary. Or that you soon would be, if you caught on to what I had. I didn't realize I'd been so obvious."

"No worries," Tamsin said. "How could I not be interested in the discovery of a manuscript? In fact, my graduate studies are being paid for by the owner of a bookshop in Edinburgh that specializes in Stevenson."

"Henry did send the emails that disappeared from your laptop and cloud storage," Nina said.

"Tamsin," Scarlett said. "You backed up everything else on flash drives, in addition to your cloud storage. Why not those emails? That did make us wonder."

"And by 'wonder,' she means 'suspect,'" Allie said.

"Who among us backs up everything they should?" Tamsin asked. "They were in the cloud, and they weren't part of my research. I was lazy."

Nina stood up and took a paper from a folder. "I'd like to read something. It's from Andy and me, but it's official because Chief Rodriguez signed it." She cleared her throat. "For quick action under cover of condor hisses, snorts, and whomping great wingbeats, that helped her take down our man, we hereby award the Order of the Scarlet Condor to Scarlett McCormick."

Her friends broke into applause, and Scarlett almost burst into tears. Then it hit her: the condors had looked Henry in the eye, and he'd run away. And suddenly, his eyes ceased to hold power over her.

As Quartz ate a small piece of chocolate pie for dessert, he told the group what he'd spent his time mulling over in the cave.

"That uninterrupted time did the trick. Thank goodness I didn't have the diary with me, or Henry would have gotten it, but I did have the clues with me." He tapped his temple. "I know where the manuscript is."

The next Saturday, the group went to Left Field Farm to watch Quartz retrieve the manuscript. Sophie, Adam, and Rylla welcomed them. In a nice surprise for Quartz, Tamsin had brought Virgil.

Quartz pumped Virgil's hand. "So good to see you again. Not many beat me at my own game of good stories and tall tales."

Virgil tipped his fishing hat to Sophie. "Nice to see you again too."

"Now, gather around, all of you," Quartz said. "I'll make an admission that most of you are far brighter than I am. You would have solved the riddle in the clues immediately. See for yourselves." He passed papers around.

Scarlett and Luke shared one, and she saw the clues she'd read in the diary at Virgil's.

Cluse to ore treshur
Done go in winder
Kip yor feed dry
Sos yu done cry
An yu chant bee sore
When yu reed ore store

"Ore is the mine," Allie said.

"Feed dry is the barn," Winnie said.

"If bee sore means a beehive," Sophie said, "my hives aren't the originals."

"All wrong, I'm afraid," Quartz said. "But I know something you don't. These 'riddles' were written by two little girls who'd barely learned to read and write. Their spelling adds to the puzzle. 'Ore' is our, 'winder' winter, 'feed' feet, 'chant' shan't, 'bee sore' be sorry, 'reed ore store' read our story."

"Ced ora a mud," Sophie said.

"Ms. Morata," Quartz said. "If you will take my arm, I'll escort you. Not in winter, and we won't get our feet wet. But if we go to your spring and into your springhouse, we should find a treasure—a Stevenson story."

Tamsin helped Virgil over the rough ground.

Winnie walked with them. "You two know each other?"

"We have a mutual fondness for Stevenson," Tamsin said.

"She came to visit me," Virgil said. "So did you. I haven't forgotten that. In fact, I have something for you." He dug in his pocket and handed her an antique mechanical burglar alarm. "I had two."

Winnie kissed his cheek.

"What's your guess today?" Rylla asked, falling into step beside Scarlett and Luke.

"Can I clear up a loose end first?"

"As a reward for finding Quartz, sure."

"The morning after Quartz disappeared, you were at the museum and left suddenly. Where did you go?"

"Text from Adam. He saw the error of his ways and decided not to break up after all."

"Is that why he skipped work that day?" Scarlett asked.

"Yep."

Scarlett frowned. "When we had our rattlesnake encounter, it sounded like you two hadn't gotten back together."

"You probably don't tell me everything about your love life either."

"You are so—"

"Cool?" Rylla supplied.

"Cool, yes. Hey, speaking of love, I got within fifteen or twenty feet of two condors in the wild."

Rylla grabbed Scarlett's arm. "You didn't."

"I did. They hissed, snorted, took off, circled around, and came back." Scarlett fluttered her hand on her heart. "I think I'm in love with them."

"Okay, toss out the reward for finding Quartz. For seeing condors, you deserve to know the name of my favorite bird. Ready? Violet-green swallow."

They'd arrived at the springhouse, and Quartz heard Rylla.

"I heard violet-green swallows before sunup each morning from the cave. They gave me hope."

"The brickwork's been patched over the years," Sophie said, "but the patch in the far corner appears oldest and least necessary. What do you think?"

"What I always think," Quartz said. "Around every corner lies the possibility of treasure."

Adam and Luke examined the corner patch and discovered a veneer of plaster over a metal box. They handed it to Quartz.

Quartz took a deep breath, opened the box, and lifted out a parcel wrapped in waterproof canvas. Inside was a manuscript. He had tears in his eyes as he presented it to Sophie. "It's part of your property, so it's rightfully yours. I was in it for the treasure hunt, so I've accomplished what I set out to do."

Tamsin offered to help Sophie sell it. "If that's what you decide to do. It's worth quite a lot."

Sophie studied the farm, the new hole in the wall of her springhouse. "The money would help, but the manuscript should stay in the community where it was written. I don't know what to do."

"I have a suggestion," Scarlett said. "If you decide to sell it, the Reed Museum would love to buy it. That way it will remain local, but anyone who wants to can see and enjoy it."

"I accept," Sophie said. "I can't think of a better place for it. But first, if they agree to take very good care of it, Quartz and Tamsin deserve time with it. Quartz because we wouldn't have it without him, and Tamsin for her research. Does that suit everyone?"

From the cheers, it was obvious that it did.

After supper that night, which Scarlett and Luke ate in front of a fire in her fireplace, she leaned her head against his shoulder. "Greta and Hal seemed kind of sad when Quartz said he'd be heading home tomorrow."

Luke laughed. "And then a bit taken aback when he said he'd be back for the trial."

"Sophie was a surprise, wasn't she? Inviting Quartz to stay at the farm was a nice gesture."

"The least she could do, considering what he did for her," Luke said. "But yes, a nice gesture."

"The closure of finding Billy's remains in the mine lifted a cloud from her life," Scarlett said. "She and Rylla and Adam were obviously comfortable and happy together. I like that. And your idea for getting to know Adam must have worked. You guys looked chummy today at the farm."

"Yeah, you learn a lot about someone when you're dangling from the end of a rope."

"About that." Scarlett sat up. "Do you know that I was terrified about you spelunking into that mine with him? And in retrospect, I might even be upset with you. You didn't know enough about him to take that kind of risk."

"Says she who laughed at rattlesnakes and took down a kidnapper."

"Fair point." Scarlett leaned against him again. "So what did you learn about Adam?"

"He's a good, brave man."

"I believe it, but simply talking isn't the only way to learn something about someone or yourself." Scarlett gazed into his eyes—deep, brown, steady, warm. Above all, caring. "Do you want to know what I learned by being terrified and possibly upset?"

"What?"

"That I don't ever want to lose you."

Cleo butted her head against Luke's knee and meowed.

Scarlett laughed. "That goes for Cleo too."

YOUR FEEDBACK MEANS A LOT TO US!

Up to this point, we've been doing all the writing. Now it's *your* turn!

Tell us what you think about this book, the characters, the bad guy, or anything else you'd like to share with us about this series. We can't wait to hear from *you*!

Log on to give us your feedback at:
https://www.surveymonkey.com/r/MuseumMysteries

Annie's FICTION